Step by Step Theater

Step by Step Theater

Creating Plays for Class Presentation

by Greg Thompson

Fearon Teacher Aids
Carthage, Illinois

Designed by: Rose Sheifer
Illustrations by: Duane Bibby

ISBN 0-8224-6348-2

Printed in the United States of America
1. 9 8 7 6

CONTENTS

Introduction 7

The Plays 11
- The Lion and the Mouse 13
- The Fishermen Who Could Not Count 17
- The Shepherd Boy and the Wolf 21
- The City Mice and the Country Mice 27
- The Wolf and the Little Kids 33
- Monkey See, Monkey Do 39
- Belling the Cat 43
- The Little Red Hen 49
- The Tortoise and the Hare 55

Costumes and Props Directions 61

Patterns 80

INTRODUCTION

It is not done willingly.

Most of us are filled with dread at the thought of it.

Others simply won't do it.

"It" is putting on a play.

Now there is an easy way. You won't have to resort to making your students stand in front of the room—books in hand—and read a play. And you won't have to reserve two months of curriculum and patience putting spit and polish into an extravaganza, using the threat of a lost recess as motivation.

This is the easy way. It requires less planning, less rehearsing, less costuming, and less frustration. It increases children's comprehension skills and their ability to follow directions, enhances self-confidence, and provides opportunities to learn to work together as a group.

How Is This Approach Different?

Step by Step Theater gives you a collection of stories to choose from, movement exercises to teach the actions of the play, a narrative script that teaches comprehension rather than memorization, and easily duplicated patterns to provide costumes and props.

Why Are These Stories Special?

The stories collected here are chosen because they have groups of characters who move and speak together. Because the students are playing identical characters, they learn from each other and are cued by each other. And when it is easier to learn what to do and say, less rehearsal time is needed.

There Are Acting Lessons

Before learning what to say, your students learn how to move like the characters and where to move during the story. These exercises are done by all class members, so everyone learns about each character. Marching, crawling, running, or swaggering, your children will turn into the characters in the story.

You Don't Give Your Students a Script?

Your students do not have to carry a script around with them. They won't have to feel tied to memorizing the lines perfectly; with this method they instead focus on learning the sequence of the story and the natural response to the situation. Using the narrative script, you feed your actors the lines during initial rehearsals, letting them repeat or paraphrase. Having already listened to the story, practiced the movements of the characters, and acted out the story while listening to you tell it, the children are familiar with what the characters are supposed to say.

And I Won't Have to Spend Nights Sewing Costumes?

At the end of the book you'll find blackline masters for the necessary costumes and props. Because your students are making their own costumes, this becomes an easily followed art lesson, using school supplies. ❧

How to Use This Book Step by Step

Introducing and Reading the Story

The stories in this book are available as picture books or in anthologies in your library. After reading the story to your students, review the sequence of events with them. Paraphrase both the actions and words of the characters—the same process you will use to practice the play. As much as possible, let your students provide the responses during this review. This review can be a quick synopsis or take as long as it took to read the story. But it is an essential step because you are building your students' understanding of the sequence of actions and familiarizing them with the logical responses of the characters.

After you have reviewed the story, see if your students can list the characters. This can be done verbally, on the board, or on paper at their seats. This exercise motivates them to review the storyline again as they remember who is in the beginning of the story, who is in it throughout, who comes in the middle of the plot, and who is predominant at the conclusion.

Setting the Stage

Before going any further, you must decide where you are going to perform and how that area should be adapted to the story. This step will give you an idea of the space you will need. The story might need two different areas or something for actors to hide behind during part of the story. You may want your students to think through the story one more time to come up with a list of essential props and scenery. In this book, these items are kept to a bare minimum: only props that are necessary to the story and scenery that is needed to conceal actors or activities from the audience.

Once you have defined the necessary space and scenery, you are ready to guide your students in different directions during the movement exercises.

Practicing the Movement Exercises

After having analyzed the story, the children are ready to become the characters. Once they are comfortable with how and where to move, they will be better able to assimilate what to say and when to say it.

Before embarking on this step, you need to first become familiar with the narrative script and movement exercises yourself, so that you will not have to be too dependent on reading while directing your young actors.

Having done this, you must select an area that will give enough room for your students to practice freely without being confined by desks and chairs. Gymnasiums, multipurpose rooms, cafeterias, and even the playground are good locations. Later, when practicing in your classroom space or on a stage, your actors will be able to confine themselves to the space. But at first you want to give them room to practice the body movements until they become comfortable.

The movements are done separately at first; the students practice moving in a certain manner or pantomiming a certain behavior. Then, having explored each movement, read through the narrative script and let the students make the appropriate movements for each character and behavior as it appears. This ensures that all students can perform all parts and increases their familiarity with the storyline as they become each character in the story.

Don't hesitate to repeat the movement exercises at any time. The more comfortable your students become with the actions of the play, the more they will free-play the experience.

This movement practice also gives you a chance to see who shines. It is for this reason that choosing or assigning parts should take place after the movement exercises have been explored.

Using a Narrative Script

The "script" is more like a story than like a traditional script. It is not meant to be a piece of paper for the students to be tied to during rehearsals. It is a tool for you to use to provide dialogue and to keep the story moving.

During rehearsals, especially initial rehearsals, read the narrative script and allow your actors to move to the areas designated during the movement exercises. When it is time for them to speak, direct them in what to say, using the lines provided. During later rehearsals, prompt them as necessary, but don't be surprised when they begin paraphrasing the content. This is a sure indication that you are on your way.

If at any time during rehearsals—or even performance—the actors come up against a blank wall, use the lines to prompt them. After all, this isn't professional theater. You don't want the storyline to be slowed, because a break in the story is embarrassing to the actors. If your actors ever forget where they are supposed to be going or what they are supposed to be doing, read the narrative. This is why the "script" is written as a narrative. It won't take long before the action is running back on track.

Making Costumes and Props

The majority of costumes for these plays are in the form of masks. The faces are easily duplicated onto construction paper to be colored with crayons or felt-tip pens or painted. Some require cutting and pasting of shapes. The instructions are given for each, but feel free to limit or expand the decorations as you see fit. It is suggested that masks be mounted on a tagboard strip that is first stapled to fit the child's head size and then stapled to the mask.

If the students make props for the play (such as the fish for *The Fishermen Who Could Not Count*), stress that though someone else may use their prop during the play, it will be returned to them and they will be able to take it home.

Bushes appear as props over and over in the stories. To save time, make them out of something durable so they can be used in the other plays. Making bushes once beats making bushes five times. ❧

Anything Else Before Getting Started?

The plays used here are meant to be put on anywhere. Don't feel limited by your surroundings. They have been performed on stages, in classrooms, and in public parks.

With class sizes being what they are, most classes should be divided into two performing groups for two audiences. Each group learns from watching their classmates rehearsing and provides good feedback when asked what they liked best about the rehearsal they watched.

These plays can be produced in a short time. They can be done in as little time as a week, if worked on each day. Or they can be stretched out over two weeks.

And one last but very important point: don't forget to enjoy the experience. Your purpose is to give your students a taste of performing and to learn the steps to putting on a play. ❧

THE PLAYS

The Lion and the Mouse

The Fishermen Who Could Not Count

The Shepherd Boy and the Wolf

The City Mice and the Country Mice

The Wolf and the Little Kids

Monkey See, Monkey Do

Belling the Cat

The Little Red Hen

The Tortoise and the Hare

The Lion and the Mouse

This well-known tale by Aesop appeals to all. It reaffirms our hope that the little guy can make a big difference when put to the test. The story is easily adapted for a classroom-size cast by multiplying the number of mice. One mouse is caught by the lion; the others plead for that mouse's sake; together, they all save the lion's life.

THE PLAY

In back of a large clearing are bushes, and behind these bushes, a band of mice is hidden.

The lion enters, roaring, "Roar. I think I'll take a nap. Roar." The lion lies down in the middle of the clearing. He sleeps.

The mice enter on tiptoe, squeaking, "Eee-eee-eee." The mice make a circle around the lion and dance. With each step they take, the mice squeak. In the dance, they follow each other around the circle: 1, 2, 3, 4, 5, 6, 7, 8, 9, 10—turn—1, 2, 3, 4, 5, 6, 7, 8, 9, 10—turn.

As the dance continues, the lion awakes but does not move. He watches and waits. Then, with a mighty roar, he grabs one of the mice.

The other mice, frightened, run back to their hiding places, squeaking.

The captured mouse, swaying back and forth in the clutches of the lion, moans, "I wish I had never come here."

The lion roars.

Again, the mouse moans, "I wish I had never come here."

Again, the lion roars.

Again, the mouse moans, "I wish I had never come here."

And again, the lion roars.

The mice, peering from their hiding place, plead for the life of their fellow mouse. "Please let her go. Please let her go. Please let her go."

The lion roars and asks, "Why should I?"

The mice reply, "Because you are so big. It isn't fair. Please let her go."

The lion roars and asks again, "Why should I?"

The mice reply, "Because she wouldn't taste good. Please let her go."

The lion again roars and once again asks, "Why should I?"

The mice reply, "Because someday she may help you if you're in trouble. Please let her go."

The lion laughs, "Ha, ha, ha. She will help me? Ha, ha, ha. Very well. I will let her go."

The lion releases his grip, and the mouse returns to her friends, who thank the lion: "Thank you. Thank you. Thank you." The mice retreat to their hiding places. The lion returns to the middle of the clearing, lies down, and resumes his sleep.

The hunters enter, carrying a net and chanting in syncopation, "Hunting for lion. Hunting for lion. Hunting for lion. Hunting for lion." They stop, turn to each other, and fingers to their mouths, whisper, "Shhh." They resume their march. "Hunting for lion. Hunting for lion. Hunting for lion. Hunting for lion." They stop, point to the lion, turn to each other, and, fingers to their mouths, whisper, "Shhh."

The hunters tiptoe up to the sleeping lion until they are in back of him. Then they throw the net over him and step back, while the lion thrashes and roars. Soon, the lion, realizing he is trapped, stops fighting and lies down. The hunters, overjoyed, jump up and down, crying, "We did it! We did it! We did it!" Then, turning to one another, they say, "Let's go get the others." The hunters leave the same way they came in.

The lion roars three times: "Roar! Roar! Roar!"

From behind the bushes, the mice squeak, "Eee-eee-eee. It's the lion. He's trapped. Let's help him." The mice form a circle around the net and use their teeth and paws to gnaw away at the net.

As the mice work to free their friend, the chant of the hunters can be heard in the distance: "Hunting for lion. Hunting for lion. Hunting for lion. Hunting for lion."

Closer and closer comes the sound. Finally, as the hunters approach, the mice free the lion. The lion stands up and roars! The hunters scream in fright and flee.

The mice sit down around the lion, who pats each one on the head and says, "You saved my life. Thank you. Thank you. Thank you." Then, turning to the audience, he and all the mice say together, "Little friends can be *big* friends." ❧

Setting the Stage

All the action of this play takes place in one area. You need a space large enough for your particular number of mice to dance in a circle around the sleeping lion.

Bushes are set up in a semicircle in the background in clumps of three and four, with enough room behind for the mice to hide.

The hunters, with their comical march, need room for an entrance. This could be from the back of the room or from some hidden spot off the stage area.

Movement Exercises

LIONS

Walk. First, have everyone practice how a lion would swagger as it walks, taking big steps from side to side and swaying its shoulders back and forth. March the lions around, swaggering proudly with each step.

Roar. Have your lions take a mighty stance, with feet spread apart and elbows out, ready to roar. Coach your lions to move their heads when roaring, letting their mouths point toward the ceiling, and lead in an S-shaped motion.

Walk and Roar. Now march the lions around again, emphasizing the swagger. Use a clapping rhythm to ensure big steps. After eight steps or claps, signal them to roar. Help them to remember the wide stance and the motion of the head as they roar. Do this until the pattern is comfortable for them.

MICE

Walk. Though the mice may in fact be the same size as the lion, they must appear to be smaller, and it is this appearance they must practice. Have the class begin by hunching down, with shoulders pulled up and "paws" leading their movements. Direct them to hold their hands together in front of their mouths. Have them tiptoe in a large circle, using this hunched-over position. Unlike the lion, who uses large steps, the mice should take very small and quick steps as they move. As you count to ten, have them take a step to each beat. After ten steps in one direction, tell them to stop, turn, and go ten steps in the other direction.

Squeak. When they stop to turn, have them practice their squeaks. Instruct them to use their highest voices while squeaking, "Eee-eee-eee." To make them even more mouselike when squeaking, have them turn to the closest mouse and squeak at it.

HUNTERS

March. Now, it is time for everyone to turn into hunters. Have the children crouch low with one hand over their brow like a sailor, sweeping the horizon as they march. Pair them and have them march as close behind their partner as they can. If they can, it will be more comical if they begin this march using the same foot. Once this is comfortable, combine partners so there are lines of four marching.

Chant. To practice the chant, begin by clapping a four-count rhythm and counting, 1-2-3-4. Next, insert the chant "hunting for lion" into this rhythm, while maintaining the clapping. To form a syncopated rhythm, the word *hunting* should be finished by the time you clap 2, the word *for* inserted in the pause between 2 and 3, and the word *lion* stretched over counts 3 and 4. Try it. See what they can do.

March and Chant. Now put the march and the chant together. Remind your students to crouch and hold a hand above their brow as they chant, "Hunting for lion. Hunting for lion. Hunting for lion. Hunting for lion." Then, they stop, turn, and, finger to mouth, whisper, "Shhh." Repeat over and over as they hunt for the lion. The longer the march of these hunters during performance, the more comical this sequence will appear.

Play Read-through

You are now ready to read the play and let the children all take on each part: the lion entering, the mice dancing and then pleading, and the hunters marching and chanting. Remember, this is only an exercise to let the children get the feel of the characters. It's not as important that it look like a play to you as that it feel like a story to the children.

Costumes and Props

- ❏ Mouse masks (see pp. 76, 92)
- ❏ Lion mask (see pp. 75, 90)
- ❏ Caps for hunters (see pp. 71, 81)
- ❏ Net (see p. 67)
- ❏ Bushes (see p. 64)

The Fishermen Who Could Not Count

Variations of the story of the failure to count oneself are told throughout Northern Europe, India, Russia, China, and many other countries. Children love the story because they can solve the mystery without an adult having to explain it for them. So the audience is happy. And your actors will have a good time, since what child doesn't have fun playing the part of someone who isn't very smart, a role seldom encouraged at school. The story adapts easily as a classroom play because it can be expanded to fit any number. For the purpose of this narrative, 12 fishermen are used.

THE PLAY

As the story begins, from the back of the room the lead fisherman says, in a loud voice, "Let's go fishing." The fishermen enter in a line. They are marching to the river.

As they survey the river, the first four choose their location, saying, "Here's a good spot." The next four choose their place. "Here's a good spot." The next four choose. "Here's a good spot."

As they fish, pulling fish "out" of the river, they sing:

I've Been Fishing On The River
(to the tune of "I've Been Working On The Railroad")

I've been fishing on the river,
All the livelong day,
I've been fishing on the river,
Just to pass the time away.
Can't you hear the river rolling,
Rolling so fast to the sea.
Can't you see the fish a-jumping,
Ready to come home with me.
I love to fish.
I love to fish.
I love to fish all day-ay-ay.
I love to fish.
I love to fish
I love to fish all day.

By this time, the fishermen should have "caught" all the fish in the river. The leader calls, "It's time to go home. Get your fish and line up." Once the fishermen are lined up, the leader says, "Are we all here? I hope no one fell into the river and drowned. I will count and see."

The leader walks behind the line and counts, touching each fisherman's pole as he counts: "1, 2, 3, 4, 5, 6, 7, 8, 9, 10, 11! There were 12 of us when we came out. Oh no! One of us has drowned in the river! Boo-hoo, boo-hoo, boo-hoo." He joins the end of the line as the other fishermen cry with him.

Now, whoever is at the front of the line stops the crying, saying, "Wait! I will count." Walking behind, touching each one's fishing pole, he counts, "1, 2, 3, 4, 5, 6, 7, 8, 9, 10, 11! Oh no! One of us has drowned in the river! Boo-hoo, boo-hoo, boo-hoo." He joins the end of the line as the others join the crying.

Whoever is at the front of the line again stops the crying, by saying, "Wait! I will count." Like the first, he walks behind the line and counts, touching each fishing pole as he counts, "1, 2, 3, 4, 5, 6, 7, 8, 9, 10, 11! Oh no! One of us has drowned in the river! Boo-hoo, boo-hoo, boo-hoo." And like the first, he joins the end of the line as they all cry together.

In the midst of this foolishness, our hero comes from the back of the room. He walks up to the crying fishermen and quiets them. "Stop your crying. What's the matter?"

The first in line explains, "One of us has drowned in the river. There were 12 of us when we came out and now there are only 11. Watch." And he counts, walking behind, touching each fishing pole as he counts. "1,2,3,4,5,6,7,8,9,10,11! One of us has drowned in the river! Boo-hoo, boo-hoo, boo-hoo." He now joins the end of the line of crying fishermen.

The hero turns to the audience, smiles knowingly, and shakes his head at their foolishness. Turning back to the fishermen, he stops their crying. "Wait! I think I can help. If I can find the one who is lost, will you stop crying?" And right down the line each fisherman replies, "Yes!"

The hero stands in front of the line of fishermen, waves his fishing pole over them, and says,

Abra-ca-dabra,

One, two, three.

Bring the fisherman

Back to me.

"Now let's see if it worked." The hero walks behind the fishermen, touching each fishing pole as he counts, "1, 2, 3, 4, 5, 6, 7, 8, 9, 10, 11, 12! You are all here."

The fishermen turn to one another and, waving their hands and fish in the air, cheer the return of their lost brother: "Hurray, hurray!" Someone yells, "Three cheers! Hip, hip, hurray! Hip, hip, hurray! Hip, hip, hurray!"

The hero stands in the front of the line, and the fishermen thank him as they pass, saying, "Thank you. Thank you so much. Thank you." The fishermen march off home, singing "I've Been Fishing On The River." The hero stands and waves. ❧

Setting the Stage

The play takes place in one large area where a river flows through. If you've made the bushes for another play, they can add a nice bit of scenery, but are not essential for any part of this story. The actors enter from the back of the room, so there must be room for them, as they will exit the same way. The hero needs to be hidden offstage or in the back of the room during the first half of the story.

Movement Exercises

FISHERMEN

March. One of the attractions of the fishermen is how silly they are. To capitalize on this, have your class practice marching for the opening sequence of the march to the river. You want them marching together as close as they successfully can. So start them in pairs—one in back of the other—marching to a clapping rhythm. Change the clapping rhythm to left-right, left-right, left-right. Begin merging the pairs of marchers as they become more comfortable marching so closely together.

Arm Swinging. Once you have a line of close-stepping marchers, show them how to exaggerate their arm swinging. Because they will be carrying fishing poles in the play, have them begin to practice with one arm pulled close to their chest, while swinging the other. Once the poles are made, you may want to have them practice marching again.

Fishing. Your fishermen will also need practice with the poles so that their casting is overhead and not to the side where someone may be in the way. For now, show them how to swing the "fishing pole" overhead and pantomime waiting for a fish to bite. Use your face to show excitement as you realize you have caught one. Reach down to the "river" and pull out your prize, set it down, and begin the process over again. Now your students are ready to begin fishing.

Lining Up. Now that they are adept at fishing, it's time for the silliness of the play. With the children spread out and fishing, have them practice getting in a line to be counted. Use the line from the play, "It's time to go home. Get your fish and line up." You want them in a line standing beside each other. Practice this several times.

HERO

Magic. Demonstrate for your children how the hero waves his fishing pole over the fishermen. Use your best flourish and sweeping arm movements. Have them practice this while repeating the "magic incantation":

Abra-ca-dabra,
One, two, three.
Bring the fisherman
Back to me.

Play Read-through

At this point read the play to the class, having them take on all parts: marching to the river, fishing, standing in line to be counted by the first fisherman in line, becoming the hero, saying the magic words, rejoicing on finding the lost fisherman, and marching back home.

Costumes and Props

- ❑ Caps (see pp. 71, 81)
- ❑ Fish (see pp. 64, 82)
- ❑ Fishing Poles (see p. 65)
- ❑ The River (see p. 68)

The Shepherd Boy and the Wolf

This story by Aesop has the child's "Sense of Right and Wrong" seal of approval. Children recognize someone who is taking advantage by lying, and they can't help but agree that the shepherd boy receives his just deserts. This story uses two choruses, both adaptable to your class size: the sheep and the villagers. The simple phrasing and repetition of action will facilitate your production. And after this project, no one could say that you're not teaching your students and your audience to be upstanding citizens.

The Play

Our story begins in a meadow where a shepherd boy is walking among his flock of sheep, who are contentedly grazing and "maa-ing." The villagers are busy painting, building, sweeping, and planting gardens.

The shepherd boy pats one of the sheep on the head and says, "You're a good sheep." The happy sheep bleats, "Maa." The shepherd boy walks over to another sheep, pats it on the head, and says, "You're a good sheep." The sheep replies, "Maa." He pats another sheep on the head and says, "You're a good sheep." The sheep responds, "Maa."

Frowning, the boy sighs and says, "This is boring." Snapping his fingers, he says, "I know what I'll do. I'll pretend there's a wolf." He puts his hands to his mouth and calls, "Wolf! Wolf! Help! Help!" The sheep, not understanding boy-talk, look at him while he yells. The shepherd boy turns to them, scrunches up his shoulders, puts his finger up to his mouth, and whispers, "Shhh." He then turns back to the village and yells, "Wolf! Wolf! Help! Help!"

The villagers, hearing the shepherd boy's pleas, shake each other, point to where the meadow is, and, carrying their work tools with them, run to the aid of the shepherd boy and the sheep. They are shaking their tools above their heads as they arrive, crying, "Where's the wolf? Where's the wolf?" Looking around them, they turn to their neighbors and say, "I don't see any wolf. Do you see a wolf? Where's the wolf? Where's the wolf?"

The shepherd boy, who has been in the back enjoying all the excitement, comes forward laughing and says, "There isn't any wolf. I fooled you. I fooled you." The villagers are upset because they have had to leave their work and, on top of that, they've been fooled. They each knit their brow, put one hand on their hip, and shake the forefinger of their other hand at the shepherd boy. They say, "That's not very funny. Don't cry 'wolf' if there isn't any wolf." And, shaking their heads, the villagers frown at the boy and return to their village and their work.

The shepherd boy looks on as the villagers return to work. Then he turns to his flock of sheep, who are again eating grass in the meadow, and walks among them. He pats one on the head and says, "You're a good sheep." The sheep replies, "Maa." Turning to another sheep, he pats it on the head and says, "You're a good sheep." The sheep responds, "Maa." He pats another sheep on the head and says, "You're a good sheep." The sheep bleats, "Maa."

Frowning, the boy again sighs and says, "This is boring." Snapping his fingers, he says, "I know what I'll do. I'll pretend there's a wolf again." And he calls, "Wolf! Wolf! Help! Help!" scrunching up his shoulders, he turns to the sheep, puts his finger to his mouth and whispers, "Shhh." Then he turns back toward the village and resumes shouting, "Wolf! Wolf! Help! Help!"

The villagers, shaking each other, point to where the meadow is, and, carrying their tools with them, run to the aid of the shepherd boy and the sheep. They are shaking their tools above their heads as they arrive, crying, "Where's the wolf? Where's the wolf?" Looking around them, they turn to their neighbors and say, "I don't see any wolf. Do you see a wolf? Where's the wolf? Where's the wolf?"

The shepherd boy, who has been in the back, comes forward laughing and says, "There isn't any wolf. I fooled you. I fooled you again." The villagers upset at being fooled a second time, each knit their brow, put one hand on their hip, and shake the forefinger of their other hand at the shepherd boy. They say, "That is the second time you have fooled us. It's not funny. Don't cry 'wolf' if there isn't any wolf." And shaking their heads, the villagers frown at the boy and return to their village and their work.

The shepherd boy watches the villagers return to work, not seeing a real wolf slinking out from the bushes where he has been hidden. The wolf begins to circle the flock of sheep, who move closer to the shepherd boy.

The shepherd boy, not seeing the wolf, returns to his job, patting a sheep on the head and saying, "You're a good sheep." The sheep responds, "Maa." The wolf moves closer to the shepherd boy. The shepherd boy turns to another sheep, pats it on the head and says, "You're a good sheep." The sheep bleats, "Maa." The wolf moves right next to the shepherd boy. The shepherd boy absently turns to the wolf, pats it on the head and says, "You're a good wolf." He stares and says, "Wolf?" Suddenly, he realizes the trouble he is in. Turning to the village, he shouts, "Wolf! Wolf! Help! Help!"

The wolf begins to nip at the heels of the sheep, causing them to "Maa" in a worried way. The shepherd boy continues yelling, "Wolf! Wolf! Help! Help!" The sheep, "maa-ing" excitedly, begin to scatter, looking for a way out of the meadow and out of the wolf's reach.

Meanwhile, the villagers, shaking each other, point to where the meadow is and say to each other, "Listen to that silly boy. He is crying 'wolf' again." Then, one by one, they say, "I'm not going." "I'm not going." "I'm not going."

The sheep, with an excited "Maa," finally run behind the bushes to get away from the wolf. As the boy continues to cry, "Wolf! Wolf! Help! Help!" the wolf runs behind the bushes, too.

The villagers all say together, "We don't believe him." Having lost all his sheep, the shepherd boy sits down, dejected, head in hands.

Two of the villagers carry the lesson of the story, written as a sign, to the center of the stage. The other villagers look on, and they all read the sign: "People won't believe someone who always tells lies." ❧

Setting the Stage

This story requires two areas: the meadow and the village. These need to be separated, as the villagers are able to hear the cries for help but are not able to see what is going on until too late. A spot in the back or to the side of the classroom can be designated as the village. If you are using a stage, you might place the meadow onstage and the village on the floor in front of the stage.

The wolf needs to be hidden during the first part of the story. At the end, the sheep need a place to hide after fleeing from the wolf. The bushes provide an answer to both problems. Set them up at the back of the meadow with enough room behind for the sheep to stay for the last few minutes of the story.

Movement Exercises

The parts of the sheep and wolf are the most strenuous, so begin and end your movement exercises with their parts, interspersed with the parts of the villagers.

SHEEP

To turn your students into sheep, have them first get down on hands and knees. Help them develop a rhythm by counting from 1 to 6 as they move. On the count of 6, have them practice bleating. The pattern is 1-2-3-4-5-6-MAAA.

Because their faces will be covered by a mask, it is important that they convey emotion with this bleat. Instruct them to tilt their heads and bleat in a contented manner and then in a frightened one. To practice their escape from the wolf, have them raise up to a hands-and-feet stoop and then run, making sure their hands touch the floor with each step. Use the same pattern: 1-2-3-4-5-6-MAAA. Prolong the "tension" of the escape sequence of the play by having them repeat this pattern, complete with the stop every six steps to bleat.

VILLAGERS

After practicing this escape, take a break by pantomiming the jobs the villagers might have. (See p. 46 for more on pantomime.) Pantomime painting a house, reaching high to paint the tops of the windows, painting low at the base of the house, and painting a large rectangular shape that would be the frame of the door. Another village task to pantomime is building: lift boards up, hold them, and hammer. Because the villagers work during most of the play, they should occasionally step back from their work and admire it. Especially when more than one villager is painting, building, or doing any other task, they can stop to pantomime talking by pointing and shaking their heads in agreement.

Other villagers can be cooking—pouring, stirring, and smelling their creations. The village also needs people planting, hoeing, and picking their crops. And what village would be very clean without people sweeping, bending down to pick up trash for the bag they carry on their back, and shoveling up the debris they have swept. As with all the jobs, real or pantomimed, people will stop at times and talk, reprimand someone not doing their job (every village needs their sleeper), and shrug their shoulders as they return to their work.

After the entire class has practiced each profession, divide it into groups to create a village that is peopled by painters, builders, cooks, sweepers, and farmers all working simultaneously. As they go about their work, warn them you will be crying "Wolf!" That will be a signal for them to run, waving their arms, to a spot you have designated. Do this several times to turn this into a game. Or, pick a different person to cry "Wolf!" each time who has been doing a good job at their pantomime. This should encourage some good acting.

WOLF

Finally, practice the movements of the sheep, but change the bleat into a growl, and the sheep become wolves. Direct the wolves to swing their heads back and forth as they growl, take six steps to your counting, and repeat the growl.

WOLF AND SHEEP GAME

If your class is not exhausted by this exercise yet, divide them into wolves and sheep for a game. Using the same pattern of growling or "maa-ing" after every sixth step, let the wolves chase the sheep to a designated spot. A wolf can catch a sheep only by hugging it. Any sheep that make it to the spot are safe. And don't forget, it's only fair that next time the sheep can be wolves—or can turn into wolf-eating sheep!

Play Read-through

Now read the play, letting all your students play each part as it comes up. Of course, it will look a bit confusing, especially when the wolf is chasing the sheep, but your purpose is to give your students practice in the movements of the characters.

Costumes and Props

- ❑ Sheep masks (see pp. 77, 93)
- ❑ Wolf mask (see pp. 79, 95)
- ❑ Sign (see p. 69)
- ❑ Bushes (see p. 64)

Only the sheep and wolf wear masks during the performance. Let the students playing the villagers and the shepherd boy make their own sheep or wolf mask for home play.

The City Mice and the Country Mice

This story by Aesop always leads to lively discussion and decision making by students as they debate the benefits and drawbacks of city and country living. Where would they rather live? In the open countryside, living off what they could find in the fields? Or in the fancy city house, filled with rich comforts but also with danger?

In the original story, there is one mouse in the country and one in the city. To expand it, simply multiply the number in each habitat. If you divide your class into two performing groups, you might have five mice living in the country, five living in the city, and three students as those pesky dogs.

THE PLAY

The country mice are in the field in front of the bushes; some are sitting, and some are talking to one another. One mouse enters, from behind the bushes, waving a letter. This mouse gathers the others around and says, "We've had a letter. Guess who it's from?" The other mice clamor, "Tell us. Who is it from?" And the mouse replies, "It is from our cousins in the city. They are coming for a visit. Let's get our place ready." The mice busy themselves, sweeping, spreading a tablecloth on the ground, and brushing their coats and those of their neighbors.

While the country mice prepare for the big visit, the city mice in their finery emerge from behind the table and proudly begin the journey to the country. The city mice proclaim their presence, saying, "Here we are."

The country mice run up to them, enthusiastically shaking their hands or patting them on the back, saying, "Welcome. I'm so glad you're here. We're so happy to see you."

The city mice walk around the country mice's field. They turn to their country cousins and say, "So, is this where you live? Where is your house?"

The country mice laugh and say, "We have no house. We live here in the field."

The city mice look at each other and say, "Oh!" They look around and ask, "Where is your dining room?"

The country mice giggle and reply, pointing to the tablecloth spread on the ground, "We don't have a dining room. We eat right here."

The city mice look at each other and say, "Oh!" Then they look around again and ask, "Where are your bedrooms?"

The country mice laugh at this and say, "We don't have bedrooms. We sleep here." And they point around them, to the bushes in the back.

The city mice look at each other and say, "Oh!"

The country mice turn to their cousins from the city and tell them, "Sit down. Make yourselves at home. We will bring our lunch." They busy themselves, picking things from behind the bushes, while the city mice brush the floor with their paws before sitting down around the tablecloth. When the country mice have set their simple meal in front of their cousins, they sit down and say, "We are ready. I hope you like it."

The city mice turn to each other and say, "Beans and bread? This is what you eat?"

And the country mice meekly reply, "Yes."

And as the mice reach for their food and nibble at it, the city mice begin bragging about how different their life is. "You should see where we live. We live in a big house." The city mice wave their arms to show how big the house is.

Amazed, the country mice stare at their cousins and say, "Really?"

Encouraged, the city mice continue, "You should see where we live. There is a huge table covered with glasses and plates and silverware. And there are mountains of delicious food."

Surprised to learn this, the country mice say, "Really?"

And now the city mice astonish their country cousins further by telling them of their bedrooms. "You should see where we live. There are huge beds with soft covers." And they show how they pull these covers over themselves and sleep.

The country mice are more amazed than ever, as they say, "Really?"

The city mice, full of their feelings of wealth and splendor, are enthusiastic now. "Yes, it's true. You should see where we live." One of the city mice exclaims, "You should come with us now and see where we live." The other city mice agree, "Yes, come with us and see where we live."

The country mice turn and ask one another, "Should we?" "Do you think we should go?" "Let's see where they live." They turn to the city mice and chorus, "Yes, let's go and see where you live."

All the mice get up from their country meal, the city mice brushing themselves off, and the country mice putting on caps or wrapping shawls around themselves for the journey.

And so the trip begins. The city mice walk proudly in the front, while the country mice follow, looking all around them and pointing at different things they see along the way.

Upon reaching their home, the city mice stop, look around, and then invite their cousins in. They wave their arms around as they show the room to the country mice. "This is where we live."

The impressed country mice exclaim, "Wow!"

The city mice point to where the bedrooms are and say, "That is where we sleep."

Again the country mice are amazed and say, "Wow!"

The city mice then walk around the table, waving at the food spread out there. "And this is where we eat."

The country mice scamper up to the table, look at each other, and exclaim, "Wow!"

The city mice explain, "The people who own this house always have big dinners like this. They always leave food on the table for us." And one by one, the city cousins point and list the food on the table that night. "Turkey." "Gravy." "Potatoes." "Cheese." "Cakes." And they all turn to their country cousins and say, "Let's eat."

They do just that, stopping occasionally to exclaim, "Delicious." "Wonderful." "Great." And it would have been completely wonderful, but just then there is a noise. The city mice look up and freeze. They exclaim, "Stop!"

Their country cousins look up from their food and ask, "What's wrong?"

The city mice only put a finger to their lips and say, "Shhh."

At this point, dogs come barking into the room. The mice do their best to hide, and they cling to one another in fear. The dogs keep barking as they bound around the table. Then the dogs leave as quickly as they came in.

The country mice turn to their city cousins and cry, "What was that?"

The city mice brush their coats as if it were nothing and reply, "Oh, those were just the dogs. They come in sometimes."

The city mice return to the table, while the country mice turn to each other and raise their hands in bewilderment. Seeing their cousins again eating the rich food, they too return to the table.

After a few moments, one of the mice again exclaims, "Stop!" The country mice look up from their food and say, "What's wrong?" The city mice only reply, "Shhh."

And once again, as suddenly as before, their meal is interrupted as the dogs return, barking and leaping about the table. The country mice grab their city cousins and shake in terror as the dogs bound in the room, barking at everything in sight. The dogs circle the table, and finally, still barking, leave the room.

When the dogs have left, the country mice turn to their cousins and say, "We are leaving. Goodbye."

The city mice, surprised, ask together, "Why?"

And the country mice, standing together as they are ready to leave, say, "We would rather eat beans and bread in peace and quiet than eat the finest foods and live in fear." ❧

Setting the Stage

The stage for this play is divided into two areas: one for the country and one for the city. The country side is decorated with bushes; the city side has a large table, covered by a tablecloth or butcher paper on three sides. From behind this table the city mice make their entrance. The table is set with dishes and food models, if available, though they are not necessary for any part of the action. On one side of the city area is a hiding space from which the dogs of the household enter.

Movement Exercises

MICE

There are two types of mice to groom for this production, but your students must first be turned into mice before the fine points are added.

Show your students that by bending over slightly, with shoulders pulled up and hands held tightly together in front of the chest, they can appear smaller and more mouselike. Have them practice this posture while taking short and sprightly, mouselike steps and squeaking, "Eee-eee-eee."

Next, they should prepare for the visit of their city cousins. Show them how to use the same mouselike movements and sweep, spread a tablecloth, and brush themselves. Let them practice these actions.

Now it is time to turn these country mice into proud, sophisticated city mice, with chests puffed out, heads held high, and paws flicking lint off their shoulders. Have them walk proudly around the room to practice until they've reached the practice area of the country mice.

Let them remain the proud cousins of the city for a practice run-through. Speak the lines of the country mice yourself and have them react as the city mice. The next time, all students should play the country mice all the way through as you read the lines of the city mice.

The city mice are going to walk around the home of their country cousins after they enter and proclaim, "Here we are." Refer back to the narrative script for the interchange between the country mice and city mice, reminding your students of their proud carriage as they proceed through the actions and lines of the city mice.

If you have time for only one read-through, upon reaching the point of entry of the dogs, stop and reverse the roles, having the students become the country mice as you read the lines of the city mice.

DOGS

The only other characters in this play are those rambunctious dogs. Your students must now practice being the opposite of the dainty mice. They need to appear as big and ferocious as possible. This may be hard to do on all fours, but they can look bigger by occasionally jumping up and down on their back paws while they bark and run around the table.

While all your students are practicing the role of the dogs, read the lines of the mice as they enjoy their feast at the table. Have them come in barking, running on all fours, and jumping to their hearts delight as soon as the city mice whisper, "Shhh." Establish a certain number of times for the dogs to go around the table before retreating. Then have them wait quietly until the cue for their second entrance. Repeat the sequence.

Choose a few dogs, and then repeat the scene with the rest of the students as the mice at the table. Show them how mice use their paws to feed themselves, taking small and quick nibbles at their food. Take the part of the mouse who says, "Stop!" and have the other mice ask, "What's wrong?" When you signal with a "shhh," the dogs should come barking in. Instruct your mice to reach for and grab another mouse or two, bend down and shiver, knocking their knees together to show fear.

After a return to the table, followed by the dogs' repeat visit, you are ready to divide the class into parts for the first read-through.

Costumes and Props

- ❑ Mice masks (see pp. 76, 92)
- ❑ Flowers for city mice (see p. 66)
- ❑ Shawls, sweaters, caps for country mice (have students bring from home)
- ❑ Tablecloth
- ❑ Big table
- ❑ Bushes (see p. 64)

The Wolf and the Little Kids

This Grimm fairy tale is a good illustration of how grisly stories for children can be. The little goats are eaten alive, and, as if that weren't enough, the mother cuts the wolf open as he sleeps. This tale makes an exciting play and, with a few tricks, one that will leave your audience wondering, "How did they do that?"

In the original story there are seven little goats, but you can use any number you wish. If you are dividing your class into two performing groups, you might have up to twelve goats, a mother goat, and the wolf.

THE PLAY

The mother goat is standing at the back of the house, watching her children. The young goats are singing and dancing around the table.

We Are Happy Little Goats
(to the tune of "London Bridge")
We are happy little goats,
Little goats, little goats.
We are happy little goats,
Dancing all around.
(Repeat)

When they have finished their song, their mother says, "My dear children, I have to go out and get some things. I won't be gone too long. Watch out for that nasty old wolf. Don't open the door and let him into the house. Do you promise?"

Each little goat in turn replies, "I promise."

With this, the mother goat leaves the house and walks to town. The children return to singing and dancing around the table.

While they are singing, who should appear from behind one of the bushes but the wolf. He slinks to the door and, when the little goats finish their song, he knocks and says, "My dear children, I have come back. Please open the door and let me in."

The little goats turn to each other, shake their heads, and say, "Our mother doesn't have a gruff voice. You are not our mother. You are the wolf."

So the wolf goes away. The little goats sing their song and dance around the table. When they finish, the wolf has returned to the house. The wolf knocks on the door, clears his throat, and, using a high voice, says, "My dear children, I have come back. Please open the door and let me in."

But the wolf has let his paws get too close to the door, and when the little goats see them, they point and say, "Our mother doesn't have black paws. You are not our mother. You are the wolf."

Again the wolf goes away. But this time he puts flour on his paws so they will look white like the mother goat's. Not knowing how the wolf's mind works, the little goats sing their song and dance their dance. When they finish, again the wolf has returned. He knocks on the door and using his high voice again says, "My dear children. I have come back. Let me in."

The little goats, not wanting to be fooled, say, "Show us your paws so we will know you are our mother." The wolf shows his paws covered in flour to look like the mother goat's. The little goats squeal, "Yea! It is our mother!"

And with that, the little goats open the door. But it isn't their mother at all. It's the wolf! As he enters, he shouts, "I've got you now!"

In panic the goats run around the table, screaming, "Help! Help!" After running around the table three times, the goats run out of the house and behind the bushes, followed closely by the wolf. As the little goats huddle behind the bushes, the wolf draws himself up as fiercely as ever a wolf has done and again says, "I've got you now!" The wolf jumps behind the bushes to begin his feast.

From behind the bushes, there are screams from the goats and howls of delight from the wolf. Then, all is quiet. The wolf emerges, holding his stomach, and sits down next to the bushes.

Meanwhile, in the house, from under the table comes the youngest little goat. During all the chasing, it has hidden under the table and escaped the wolf. Now, it sits with its head on the table, crying.

The mother goat returns and sees the littlest goat—all alone. She asks, "What has happened? Where are your brothers and sisters?"

The little goat replies, "Mother, the wolf came into the house and chased my brothers and sisters out of the house and ate them."

The mother goat asks, "Where is that wolf now?"

And the littlest goat replies, "He's over by the bushes."

And over by the bushes, the wolf, having eaten a very large meal, has fallen asleep. The mother goat looks at him and says, "I've got an idea. Fetch my scissors and needle and thread." The little goat does as its mother has asked.

And so, the mother goat and the little goat tiptoe out of the house and over to where the wolf is sleeping off his big dinner. The mother goat leans over the wolf's stomach and says, "I think they are still alive in there. Fetch me some rocks." The little goat goes in search of rocks in back of the house.

Now the mother goat goes to work. Taking her scissors, she cuts the wolf open, and one by one, the little goats come out and stand by their mother. The mother goat puts her finger to her mouth and says, "Shhh."

By now the littlest goat has returned with the rocks. The mother goat puts the rocks in the wolf's belly and says, "Now, he won't know you aren't in there."

And with that, she takes her needle and thread and, with big strokes, sews the wolf back up. When she is finished, she whispers to her children, "Come back to the house with me." The mother goat and her children tiptoe back to the house where they peer out from the doorway to watch the wolf.

The wolf now wakes up after his long sleep. He pats his stomach and says, "Those were the best little goats I ever ate. But I am so thirsty now. I must have something to drink." The wolf rises, holding his stomach, and slowly walks to the well. When he gets there, he says, "I am so thirsty. I want a real big drink."

The wolf leans over the edge of the well, and feeling himself losing his balance, he screams "Help!" as he falls into the well.

The mother goat and her little goats run over to the well, and circling it, look down. They say together, "The wolf has drowned himself. Hurray!" And they are so happy that they form a circle in front of the bushes and sing their song. ❧

Setting the Stage

There are two stage areas for this play; one that centers around a table, representing the house the goats live in, and another with at least six bushes and a well. If you have a chart rack or something similar, this can be an effective divider between the two areas, as well as the door to the house: the door that separates the goats from the wolf.

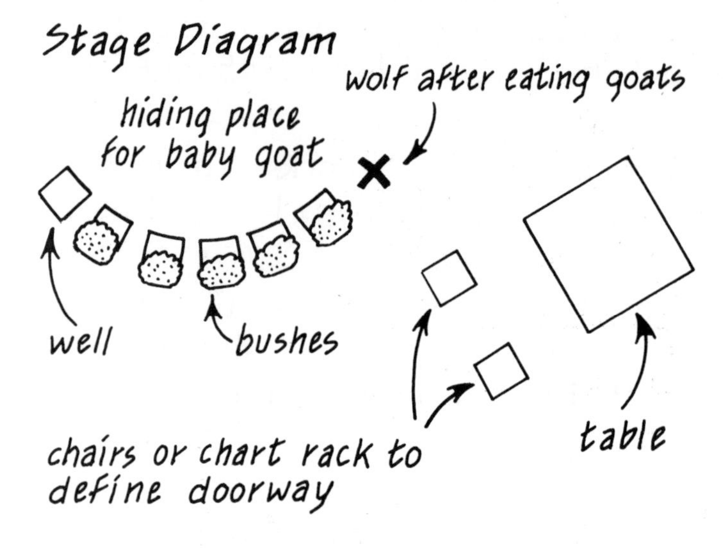

When arranging the bushes as scenery, place them in a half circle, with one chair as the well on the far end. When the little goats run behind the bushes to escape the wolf, be sure they crouch low so the audience cannot see them.

Later, after the wolf has gorged himself, have him fall asleep next to the last bush, with his back to the audience. This way, when the mother goat leans over to "cut" the wolf open, the cutting is hidden from the audience. The squeaking of the scissors will be enough to widen your audience's eyes. Then the goats that were eaten can, one by one, crawl over the wolf as they again see the light of day and the faces of the audience. The wolf's position will also be useful as the mother goat, with big strokes, sews the wolf back up.

With the well at the other end of the half circle, the wolf will have an adequate hiding place when, at the end of the story, he falls in and meets his fate.

Movement Exercises

GOATS

Prance. The first thing to teach your class is how to make convincing goats. Have them hold their "hooves" well in front of themselves and bob their heads from side to side to convey happiness with their lot in life. To practice the dance, they should be in a circle, holding their "hooves" well in front of their chests and all facing in the same direction. Show them how to prance, lifting their feet high and waving their bent arms from side to side. When they feel comfortable with this movement, see if they can sing the song at the same time. If mastering both song and dance is too advanced, sing for them as they dance in the circle. Decide how many times the song will be sung each time the goats dance around the table.

Run. Next have them practice being the goats running away from the wolf. They simply need to speed up their pace, using the same goat movements. Have one of the goats take the part of the youngest goat, who escapes. After they have run around twice, have this goat run into the middle of the circle and crouch down low as if it were under the table. Switch this part several times, allowing other goats to escape into the center of the circle.

Chase Sequence. Practice the complete chase sequence by appointing one member of the circle to be the wolf and the next person to be the leading goat. Another goat in the circle should be the littlest goat, who escapes. Designate a spot in the room to be the area of the bushes where the other goats will run to, following the lead goat and being chased by the wolf.

As the goats and wolf run in the circle, count their laps out loud. At lap two, the littlest goat runs into the center of the circle and crouches low. At lap three, the lead goat leads the other goats to the designated spot where they crouch low. They are followed by the wolf, who says, "I've got you now!" when he arrives. Practice this several times, letting different children assume the parts of the littlest goat, the lead goat, and the wolf.

WOLF

Let everyone practice the wolf's walk. He should have his elbows bent and his fingers spread as he swaggers to the house each time. Have the children cross the room, using this stance. When they get to the far end, have them pantomime the knock at the door and say, "My dear children. I've come back. Please let me in."

The last part of the play to practice in this setting is the end of the wolf. Your students can simply crawl over the chair that represents the well. Or if they have the necessary skill and if you can have a mat in back of the bushes and the well, the wolf can do a somersault over the well by doing a diving roll. If you choose to use the diving roll, practice it now. Of course, there will be no approach, so that means a slow and deliberate roll.

Play Read-through

Now read through the play, letting all your students be goats during this reading. You can be the mother goat and show them how to cut the wolf open and then sew him back up.

Costumes and Props

- ❑ Goat masks (see pp. 72, 86)
- ❑ Wolf mask (see pp.79, 95)
- ❑ Wolf's disguise (see p. 79)
- ❑ Bushes (see p. 64)
- ❑ Divider/"door"
- ❑ Chair for well
- ❑ Scissors

Monkey See, Monkey Do

Versions of this folktale are found from Egypt to England. The theme of monkeys imitating people delights children, both when animals get the better of an adult and when the adult figures out a means of getting the better of the animals. In this variation the peddler woman is selling scarves when she takes a break for lunch in the city zoo. She is the unwitting victim of the monkey's antics until she realizes that what monkeys see, monkeys do. For this adaptation the number of monkeys is limited only by the number of chairs for bushes and the size of the stage area.

THE PLAY

As the story begins, the monkeys are hidden behind the hedge of bushes. From the back the peddler woman enters, scarf over her head and a basket of scarves to sell in her hand, calling, "Pretty scarves! Pretty scarves! Get your pretty scarves!" She continues calling this refrain as she walks back and forth, "Pretty scarves! Pretty scarves! Get your pretty scarves!" She looks at her watch and says, "It's lunchtime. I think I'll eat my lunch in the city zoo."

She walks to the zoo as she continues to peddle her scarves. "Pretty scarves! Pretty scarves! Get your pretty scarves!" Upon reaching a bench in front of a hedge of bushes, she stops. "This is a good spot for my lunch." Reaching into her basket, she retrieves her lunch, sets the basket behind the bench, and sits down for her midday rest.

While the peddler woman eats, out from the bushes comes a troop of monkeys. Each monkey grabs a scarf out of the basket until all the scarves are gone. The monkeys return to their hiding place behind the hedge of bushes.

The peddler woman finishes her lunch, brushes her hands, and says, "What a good lunch. Time to get back to work." She looks behind her, picks up her basket, and cries, "My scarves! My pretty scarves! Where are my pretty scarves?" She begins looking everywhere, walking up and down the path, looking under the bench, and finally crouching down to search under the bushes.

When the peddler woman stands up, the monkeys also rise from their hiding places in the bushes. They scratch their heads and under their arms as they cry, "Ooh, ooh, ooh! Ooh, ooh, ooh!" On their heads and in their hands are the peddler woman's scarves. The monkeys have taken her scarves!

The peddler woman turns her back to the monkeys and puts her hands on the sides of her cheeks and shakes her head in worry. She says, "What will I do?" Behind her the monkeys put their hands on the sides of their cheeks and shake their heads while they chatter, "Ooh, ooh, ooh! Ooh, ooh, ooh!"

The peddler woman turns back to the monkeys and puts her hands on her waist. She shakes her head and says, "What will I do?" And the monkeys respond by putting their hands on their waists, shaking their heads, and crying, "Ooh, ooh, ooh! Ooh, ooh, ooh!"

The peddler woman takes a step back in surprise. She takes her scarf off her head and wraps it around her neck. The monkeys take their scarves and wrap them around their necks. They cry, "Ooh, ooh, ooh! Ooh, ooh, ooh!"

The peddler woman takes another step back in surprise. She takes her scarf and wraps it around her shoulders. The monkeys take their scarves and wrap them around their shoulders. They cry, "Ooh, ooh, ooh! Ooh, ooh, ooh!"

This time the peddler woman takes her scarf and wraps it around her waist. She shakes her hips back and forth. The monkeys take their scarves, wrap them around their waists, and shake their hips. They cry, "Ooh, ooh, ooh! Ooh, ooh, ooh!"

The peddler woman takes her scarf and waves it back and forth. The monkeys take their scarves and wave them back and forth. They cry, "Ooh, ooh, ooh! Ooh, ooh, ooh!"

Now the peddler woman turns and shakes her head up and down. She has figured out what to do. Turning back to the monkeys, she waves her scarf in the air once more and then throws it to the ground. The monkeys wave their scarves in the air and then throw them down. They cry, "Ooh, ooh, ooh! Ooh, ooh, ooh!"

The peddler woman picks up the scarves and puts them in her basket. The monkeys are dancing up and down at the fun they have had. They scratch their heads and under their arms. They cry, "Ooh, ooh, ooh! Ooh, ooh, ooh!"

The peddler woman walks back to her work now, calling, "Pretty scarves! Pretty scarves! Get your pretty scarves!" The monkeys wave goodbye. ❧

Setting the Stage

There is only one main stage area for this play, using the bushes as a hiding place for the monkeys. They are placed close together to form a hedge. You may decide to use as many monkeys as you have bushes, letting each monkey use the chair to stand on. Or you may use a larger number, positioning the additional monkeys in between those who will be standing on the chairs.

The peddler woman sits on a bench in the city zoo, so place a chair in front of the bushes, leaving enough room for the monkeys to sneak up and steal the woman's scarves.

The peddler woman enters and exits from the back of the stage area, so position your audience to leave room for this entrance and exit.

Movement Exercises

MONKEYS

Stance. The first phase is to turn your students into monkeys. Not too hard, you might think. First, practice a stance. Squat halfway down and cock your head to one side, practicing the monkey's call, "Ooh, ooh, ooh. Ooh, ooh, ooh." Then shrug your shoulders and let your arms hang down loosely, swaying them back and forth, again while practicing the monkey's call, "Ooh, ooh, ooh. Ooh, ooh, ooh."

Movements. Now, let's get your monkeys moving. Have them begin by crouching down low, as they would if they were hiding behind the bushes. Direct them to rise slowly, remembering to squat down, cock the head, and shrug the shoulders. Show them the classic monkey body movements of scratching the top of their heads and under the arms. Let them practice this, turning to their neighbors and showing them their monkey routine.

Imitating. Practice the actions of the peddler woman as the monkeys imitate what she does. With every motion they make, they cry, "Ooh, ooh, ooh. Ooh, ooh, ooh." First they put their hands on the sides of their cheeks and shake their heads. Then they wrap the scarves around their necks. Next they wrap the scarves around their shoulders. Then they wrap the scarves around their waists and shake their hips. Next they take the scarves and wave them over their heads. And finally they wave the scarves in the air again and throw them down to the ground.

Play Read-through

You are now ready to read the play, allowing the children to become each character as it appears: calling as the peddler woman tries to sell her scarves, becoming the monkeys, mimicking the peddler woman as she tries to retrieve her scarves, and finally, throwing the scarves down to resolve the play.

Costumes and Props

- ❑ Monkey masks (see pp. 76, 91)
- ❑ Scarves (Have the children bring these from home.)
- ❑ Basket
- ❑ Bushes (see p. 64)
- ❑ Chair for bench

Belling the Cat

This fable by Aesop tells the story of the mice who feel their troubles will be over if they can hang a bell around the neck of the cat who has been pestering them. As its lesson, "Some things are easier said than done" suggests, the story doesn't end in success for the mice.

The size of the cast of mice is adjustable. You may want to divide your class into two performing groups for two different audiences. The story can be as long—with each mouse taking a turn attempting to "bell" the cat—or short—with most of the mice passing the bell to the next mouse in line.

THE PLAY

As the play opens, a family of mice are relaxing, some sitting on chairs and reading, some on the floor and playing a game, and others standing and talking to themselves in low voices.

The quiet is broken by the shriek of a mouse offstage. "Eek!" This mouse runs across the stage, squeaking, "Eek, eek, eek!" The mouse is being chased by a cat, who is growling, "I'll get you! I'll get you!"

The mouse safely reaches the home of the mouse family, out of breath and panting. The cat growls after him, "I'll get you next time." And with that, the cat walks to the sofa, lays down, and says, "Time for a nap." And the cat falls asleep.

Meanwhile, the mouse, who has now recovered, explains to the mouse family how he came to be chased by the cat. "All I was trying to do was get a piece of cheese. I didn't hear the cat coming."

And all the mice sympathize by exclaiming, "Oh, that cat!" Each mouse in turn tells of being chased by the cat. The first mouse says, "I was almost caught by that cat." The chorus of mice responds, "Oh, that cat!" The next mouse says, "Me, too. The cat almost got me once." And the chorus responds, "Oh, that cat!" The next mouse tells his tale, "I was almost caught by that cat, too." And the chorus responds, "Oh, that cat!" Each mouse in turn tells of almost being caught by that cat, and each time, the rest of the mice respond, "Oh, that cat!"

After all the mice have told of being chased by that cat, they form a circle and turn in one direction and march while they sing.

Stop That Cat

(to the tune of "Frère Jacques")

We must stop him,
We must stop him,
Stop that cat, stop that cat.
Get him out of our lives.
Get him out of our lives.
Oh, that cat! Oh, that cat!

One of the mice says, "But what shall we do?" Another mouse proclaims, "I have an idea!" All the mice excitedly cry, "What is it?" What is your idea? Tell us! Tell us!"

The mouse points to a shiny bell and explains, "We can stop him with this bell. While the cat is asleep, one of us will hang this bell around his neck. Then whenever he moves, we'll hear him coming."

All the mice cry, "Hurray, hurray!" Then one of the mice from the back says, "But who is brave enough to hang the bell on the cat?" Everyone looks at the mouse who had the idea. That mouse puffs out its chest and says, "I am brave enough. I will do it."

And the mouse who had the idea picks up the bell and slowly creeps out of the mouse hole and tiptoes to where the cat is sleeping. The other mice line up to watch. As the mouse approaches, the cat stirs, making a small snoring noise. The mouse jumps and runs back home.

It hands the bell to the next mouse in line and says, "You do it," and goes to the end of the line. The lucky mouse with the bell puffs out its chest and says, "I am brave enough. I will do it."

And the second mouse picks up the bell and slowly creeps out of the mouse hole. The mouse tiptoes to where the cat is sleeping. As the mouse gets nearer, the cat again stirs, snores a bit, and frightens the mouse back to the hole.

This mouse hands the bell to the next in line and says, a bit out of breath, "Here. You do it." And then it goes to the end of the line. The new choice puffs out its little mouse chest, as the first two mice had done, and says proudly, "I am brave enough. I will do it."

And, as before, the third mouse meets the same fate. And so it goes. Each mouse in turn is handed the bell. Some try to tiptoe up to the cat, but become frightened and run back. Some merely pass it to the next in line, without even trying. They simply say, "Not me. I don't want to get caught by that cat." And they go to the end of the line.

Soon every mouse has had a chance, and the mouse with the idea in the first place is back at the front of the line.

Now discouraged, for no one is able to put the bell around the cat's neck, the lead mouse turns and looks at the other mice and says, "If no one here will hang the bell on the cat, we will just have to wait until some new mouse comes here who will do it."

And with that, the other mice turn to one another and agree, "Yes, we will wait for someone new to come who will stop that cat." "Yes, we will wait." "Yes, that is what we will do."

The mice begin to sing a new song:

Stop That Cat

(to the tune of "Frère Jacques")

Who will stop him,
Who will stop him,
Stop that cat, stop that cat?
Get him out of our lives,
Get him out of our lives,
Oh, that cat! Oh, that cat!

The mice return to their activities—sitting and reading, playing games, or standing and talking. They are satisfied that the solution to their problem is to wait for someone new to come who will bell the cat.

One of the mice comes to the front, carrying a sign. The mouse says, "No one ever came around who would hang the bell on the cat. And so it goes. Cats still chase mice to this very day." And, holding up the sign, the mouse reads the lesson of the story: "Some things are easier said than done." ❧

Setting the Stage

The stage is divided into two separate spaces—the mice's home and the cat's home—plus a small hiding place for the cat and one of the mice at the beginning of the story. For the mice's home, use student chairs to set up an area that resembles a living room, with chairs in random groupings. On one of the chairs or hanging on the wall is the bell. The mice's home is divided from the cat's quarters by a chart rack to go through or by two chairs set apart as an entrance to the mouse hole.

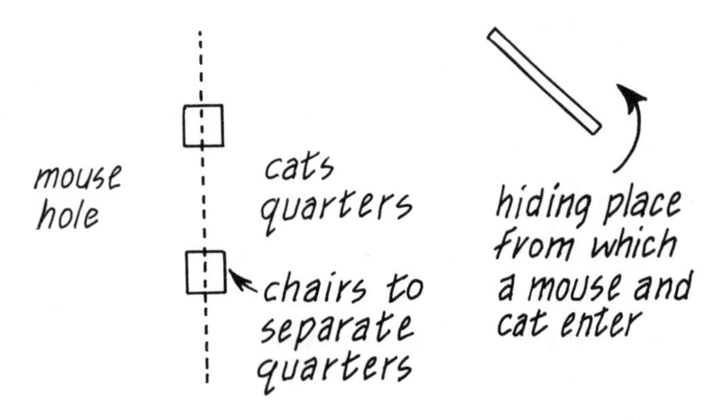

The cat's quarters contain a "sofa" made from three student chairs, covered by a blanket. On the other side of the cat's quarters is a small hiding place from which a mouse being chased by the cat enters at the beginning of the play.

Movement Exercises

PANTOMIME

Because the same movements are repeated at the beginning and end of the play, practicing being the mice at home is a good time to introduce the art of pantomime to your class. Explain that pantomime is using body movements rather than words to describe something.

Show your students how, even while sitting in a chair, a person can express different feelings. Legs may be crossed, arms may be folded, eyes may be looking around the room, or the head may be resting on the hand. Have them use these techniques to express looking bored or relaxed or even angry.

Even reading can be pantomimed. The book is held comfortably, the eyes follow the words left to right, and the pages are turned. As with all movement exercises, every student should practice pantomiming reading.

For the three or four mice playing a game on the floor, set up a gameboard or play area. The players sit around the game. They can roll dice or spin a spinner or move playing pieces. Then, of course, they each must wait while the others have their turn. And who doesn't watch to see if their opponent makes a better move and then look happy or sad, according to the spin or the roll of the dice.

And, of course, there are all the postures and gestures we use when talking to one another. Arms might be folded, fingers might be pointing, heads might be shaking yes or no.

MICE

Now that your class can pantomime these leisure-time activities, it is time to turn these actors into mice. Show them how to "shrink" into a little mouse by holding their paws tightly in front of them, bending their heads close to their paws, and pushing their shoulders up toward their ears. When they are running away from the cat, as the lead mouse does at the beginning of the story, they run on tiptoe, shrieking, "Eek, eek, eek!" Let your students practice running like a mouse back and forth to the spot that will be used as the home for this troupe of mice.

CAT

The cat must appear as large to your audience as he does to your mice. The arms must be held out from the body to show a large frame. When chasing the poor mouse, the cat should take wide steps from side to side, tilting the body into each step. While he is chasing the mouse, the cat should be saying, "I'll get you! I'll get you!" You will need to establish a point where the cat is stopped, presumably by the wall that has the entrance to the mouse hole. In this practice session, it could be a line dividing the stage area in half. When the cat reaches this point, he growls, "I'll get you next time." Then your students—as all are now pretending to be the cat—lumber back, yawn, stretch, lie down, and say, "Time for a nap."

MICE CREEPING UP ON CAT

The mice need a chance to practice creeping up on the cat to hang the bell around his neck. Each mouse uses the same series of movements: Raise a paw and say, "I am brave enough; I will do it," then puff out the chest, grab the bell with one paw, and tiptoe closer and closer to the cat. You can let your students decide how close they want to get. Some may get only a few steps out of the hole, whereas others may be poised and ready to hang the bell around the cat's neck before they run, squeaking, back to the hole and safety.

Play Read-through

Once all movements have been practiced separately, the entire play can be read to the class, letting students adopt all the parts for themselves.

Costumes and Props

- ❑ Mice masks (see pp. 76, 92)
- ❑ Cat mask (see pp. 71, 83)
- ❑ Bell (see p. 63)
- ❑ Sign (see p. 69)
- ❑ Blanket for "sofa"

The Little Red Hen

There are numerous versions of this British-American nursery tale. And there are numerous variations of the animals in the cast who will not help the little red hen. This version uses animals introduced previously in other plays. Each character in this version, though, becomes a group of characters, acting and speaking together. So, the farmyard is a haven of laziness for a small flock of sheep, a pack of dogs, and a pride of cats, who do little to help the brood of little red hens.

THE PLAY

A nice sunny morning greets the animals of the farm as the day and the story begin. The hens, always the busy workers, come onstage first. "What a nice day. Cluck. Cluck," they say as they begin pecking around the bushes.

The family of sheep enters, full of their morning meal and eager for a nice rest. They greet the hens: "Good morning, hens. What a nice day. Maa. Maa." And the sheep sit down together.

A group of dogs come in next with a "woof" and greet the other animals, "Good morning, hens. Good morning, sheep. What a nice day. Woof. Woof." And they lie down together.

The cats are the last to come into the farm scene. They greet the others, "Good morning, hens. Good morning, sheep. Good morning, dogs. What a nice day. Meow. Meow." And they sit down together.

The hens continue pecking around the farm, when they find some grains of wheat. This excites them. "Cluck, cluck, cluck. Look, look, look. Wheat! There are grains of wheat." Turning to the other animals, they say, "If we plant this, we can grow some wheat. Who will plant the grains of wheat?"

The sheep are the first to look up and answer, "Not us. Maa, maa." The dogs look up at the hens, "Not us. Woof, woof." The cats agree, "Not us. Meow, meow." And all the animals begin to sing:

Sleep, Sleep, Sleep All Day

(to the tune of "Row, Row, Row Your Boat")

Sleep, sleep, sleep all day.
That's what we will do.
Who will do the work here?
Why not you!

The hens, who have been watching this performance of laziness, look at each other, nod their heads yes, and say, "All right, we will do it." They pick up the grains of wheat and carry it in back of the bushes. Soon they reappear and go back to their tireless routine of pecking around the farm.

As the hens peck and the other animals rest, the wheat begins to grow. When the wheat has grown to its full height, the hens look up and say, "Cluck, Cluck, Cluck. Look, look, look. The wheat has grown! If we cut the wheat, we can take it to the mill. Who will cut the wheat?"

The sheep shake their heads no and say, "Not us. Maa, maa." The dogs shake their heads no and say, "Not us. Woof, woof." The cats look up from their naps and agree, shaking their heads no and saying, "Not us. Meow, meow." And all the animals begin to sing:

Sleep, sleep, sleep all day.
That's what we will do.
Who will do the work here?
Why not you!

The hens look at each other, nod their heads yes, and say, "All right, we will do it." They go back to the stalks of wheat behind the bushes and cut the wheat with scissors and put it in sacks. When this task is completed, they walk back to the other farm animals, dragging the sacks with them: "Cluck, cluck, cluck. Look, look, look. The wheat has been cut! If we take it to the mill, we can have it made into flour. Who will take the wheat to the mill?"

The sheep, as lazy as before, refuse and say, "Not us. Maa, maa." The dogs do the same, shaking their heads, "Not us. Woof, woof." The cats follow, "Not us. Meow, meow." And once again the animals sing:

Sleep, sleep, sleep all day.
That's what we will do.
Who will do the work here?
Why not you!

Having heard all this before, the hens look at each other, nod their heads yes, and say, "All right, we will do it." They pull the sacks of wheat to the mill and return in a few minutes, with the sacks now over their shoulders. Standing in front of all the animals, they say, "Cluck, cluck, cluck. Look, look, look. The wheat has been made into flour! If we make it into dough, we can bake some bread. Who will make it into dough?"

The sheep look at the hens, shake their heads no, and say, "Not us. Maa, maa." The dogs look at the hens, shake their heads no, and say, "Not us. Woof, woof." The cats look at the hens, shake their heads no, and say, "Not us. Meow, meow." And once again the animals sing:

Sleep, sleep, sleep all day.
That's what we will do.
Who will do the work here?
Why not you!

Having heard all this before, the hens look at each other, nod their heads yes, and say, "All right, we will do it." They take the sacks of flour to the table, pour some into bowls and stir and stir. Soon the dough is ready. The hens pour the dough into pans and put the pans into the oven.

While the bread is baking, the hens walk out into the farmyard and talk about what has happened. One hen says, "We found the wheat." Another says, "We planted it." Another says, "We cut the wheat." Another says, "We took it to the mill." Another says, "We made the dough." And they all say together, "We made the bread."

Just then, all the animals lift their heads and sniff, for now the air is filled with the fragrant smell of newly baked bread. The sheep are the first to speak, "We smell something good. Maa, maa." The dogs are not far behind in their appreciation. "We smell something good. Woof, woof." The cats turn to each other shaking their heads in agreement. "We smell something good. Meow, meow."

The hens return to the kitchen and pull out the pans of bread. They take these out to the farmyard. "Cluck, cluck, cluck. Look, look, look.

The flour has been made into bread! Now we can have something good to eat. Who will eat the bread?"

The sheep are the first to speak, "We will. Maa, maa." The dogs are eager to agree, "We will. Woof, woof." The cats do the same, "We will. Meow, meow."

The hens, clutching the bread close to themselves, shake their heads no for the first time and say, "No, you won't. We did all the work. You didn't do any. We will eat the bread." And the proud hens walk back to the table, as all the other animals' eyes follow and their bodies lean toward the meal they will be missing. The hens put the bread down, turn to the other animals, and sing:

Work, Work, Work All Day
(to the tune of "Row, Row, Row Your Boat")

Work, work, work all day.
We're the ones that do.
Who will eat the bread now?
No, not you! ❧

Setting the Stage

The complete stage area can be used as the sole setting for this play. The bushes should be near the back, pulled together as a hedge, with enough room behind them for the growing wheat field. To one side, place a table covered to the floor in front and on the sides with butcher paper but left open in the back for the hens to use as an oven. Place the bread, in whatever form you may decide to use, under this table. Plaster food models could be used, if available; real bread or muffins might be used; or just the pans would be enough to create the illusion.

This is one of the few plays where some players will manipulate the props. Hidden behind the bushes, they will create the illusion of the wheat growing. After the hens have planted the wheat and returned in front of the bushes with the other animals, those hidden players slowly raise the wheat above the level of the bushes.

The grains of wheat (or cracked wheat from a health store, which could be given as samples to your audience after the play) are on the front stage area before the show. Hidden behind the bushes, in addition to the students who will make the wheat grow, are scissors to cut the wheat and sacks or pillowcases stuffed with paper.

The mill can be reached by going to an offstage area, and the same sacks that hold the cut grain can be carried back holding the "flour."

Movement Exercises

HENS

Pecking. The hens, the dominant characters, are the first to appear, so begin with them. Let your students try pecking first. Show them how to push their heads forward, encouraging them to think about their chins hitting something in front of them. Let them walk around like this until it becomes easy for them.

Wings. The hens must use their hands during much of this play, so show them that the hens will hold their hands chest high, waving the elbows in front of the body in small back-and-forth movements. If any students can move their heads at the same time they are moving their elbows, point this out to the others. If doing the two movements simultaneously proves too difficult, instruct them to do one at a time and alternate head and arm movements. See if they can walk around doing the two movements.

Walk. If it's not advanced for your actors, there is one more movement that is guaranteed to bring the house down. Hens walk with a characteristic dip, bending the knees and bringing the foot up high. Using all these actions turns the hen's movements into a dance of sorts.

Clucking. See if your students can enter and move like a hen to a designated spot, using these movements. Once there, demonstrate how the hens will speak in a high voice as they say, "What a nice day!" The clucks should start at midrange and end high: "Cl-uck, cl-uck."

Because this is such a funny combination, and one the actors need to feel comfortable with, you may decide to do a read-through now, with all students acting as the hens and simply reading the parts of the other animals. This will give them a chance to enjoy how silly it all is and give you a chance to see who might make good hens.

SHEEP

To practice the part of the sheep, have your students bend down on hands and knees. Have them walk to the spot they will be settling down in, and as a comic touch, wiggle themselves before sitting down. The bleat of the sheep is quite nasal.

DOGS

Enter the dogs, who might be a bit more energetic than the sheep but just as lazy. On hands and knees, as for the sheep, show them how to kick one leg and then the other as you approach your place to sit down. After sitting, practice the low but happy "Woof, woof."

CATS

The last animal to practice is the cat. As if the song in the play were written especially for them, they enter on all fours, ever so slowly. Once they reach their spot, show them how to move their heads from side to side before reclining on their sides, leaning on an elbow. Show them how a cat licks its paws from time to time. Their voices should be as slow as their movements and have a special dip in the middle of their "Me-ow, me-ow."

Play Read-through

With reminders about how each character enters, the play can be read, letting all students adopt all characters as they appear.

Costumes and Props

- ❑ Sheep masks (see pp. 77, 93)
- ❑ Dog masks (see pp. 72, 84, 85)
- ❑ Cat masks (see pp. 71, 83)
- ❑ Little Red Hen mask (see pp. 74, 89)
- ❑ Wheat (see p. 70)
- ❑ Bushes (see p. 64)
- ❑ Sacks (for sacks of wheat, stuff sacks or pillowcases with newpaper)
- ❑ Scissors
- ❑ Table covered with butcher paper
- ❑ Bread (real or food model or just pans)
- ❑ Cracked wheat (optional)

The Tortoise and the Hare

This familiar tale by Aesop chronicles the boastfulness of the hare in his race with the tortoise. This play uses a group of hares, one to do the running, and the others to follow and contribute to the boasting. On the other side of this match is a group of intimidated animals, with the exception of one tortoise. Divide your class into two performing groups for two different audiences. The number of hares and other animals is flexible.

THE PLAY

A group of hares is gathered together with a group of other animals: cats, mice, goats, and a tortoise (and as many other kinds of animals as you want to include). They are discussing which animal is the best.

One of the hares stands in front and tells the others, "We hares are the best. We are the best animals." The other hares chime in, "Yes, yes, we're the best." The leader waves at his fellow hares and says, "We are the smartest." The other hares chorus, "Yes, yes, we're the best." The leader waves again at his brothers and sisters and says, "We are the handsomest." The other hares repeat, "Yes, yes, we're the best." The leader again waves at the other hares and declares, "We are the fastest." And the other hares agree, "Yes, yes, we're the best." The hares begin to sing:

We Are the Best
(to the tune of "Three Blind Mice")

We are the best.
We are the best.
See how we run.
See how we run.
We all run faster than any of you.
We're better-looking and smarter, too.
We wouldn't want to be any of you,
'Cuz we are the best.

The other animals have not enjoyed this boasting a bit. They turn to each other, frowning and shaking their heads. Then they turn to the hares and challenge, "You think you are the smartest?" And the hares boast together, "Yes, yes, we're the best."

The animals ask, "You think you are the handsomest?" The hares respond, "Yes, yes, we're the best."

The animals ask, "You think you are the fastest?" Again the hares boast, "Yes, yes, we're the best." And with that, all the other animals say together, "Prove it!"

The hares look at their leader, who turns to the animals and, pointing a finger at them, responds, "You want proof? All right, then. I will race with any of you to prove we are the best. Who wants to try?"

The animals turn to each other, and beginning with the first in line, each animal shakes its head no and turns to the next in line, who shakes its head and turns to the next. All down the line, the cats and mice and goats turn down the hare's challenge to race. At the end of the line is the tortoise, who slowly accepts the challenge, "I . . . will . . . race . . . you." The leader of the hares says, "All right, let's race."

The animals assemble on the far side of the starting line, with the hare and tortoise ready to run. One of the animals points to the course, saying, "Here is the race course. The first one across the finish line wins."

The other hares yell to their leader, "This will be easy." The other animals yell to the tortoise, "Do your best." And they all start the race together: "On your marks. Get set. Go!"

The tortoise starts out, slowly putting one foot in front of the other. The other animals cheer on the tortoise. "Go, tortoise, go." The hare races off the starting line, running a few steps, jumping, running a few more steps, twirling, and running some more.

The other hares follow, running and jumping behind the lead hare. The other animals remain at the starting line, cheering on the tortoise, "Go, tortoise, go."

The hares reach the bushes at the midway point, where they stop. The lead hare boasts, "Well, I guess we showed them." And the other hares chime in, "Yes, yes, we're the best."

One of the hares, carrying a sack, says, "Let's have something to eat." And the other hares agree, "Yes, yes, let's do that. Yes, yes, I'm hungry."

And so the hares spread their food out, sit down, and eat.

Meanwhile, the tortoise is struggling on. The other animals pick up their chant, "Go, tortoise, go."

The lead hare, finished with the meal, stretches and says, "Let's have a little nap. That tortoise will never catch us." The other hares agree, "Yes, yes, let's have a little nap." And with that they lay down, some resting on each other's laps, and sleep.

The tortoise passes them as they sleep, and the other animals cheer, "Go, tortoise, go." They repeat this chant as the tortoise gets nearer to the finish line. Soon this cheering wakes the hares.

"What's going on? Wake up. Wake up." They shake each other and push their leader back onto the racecourse. And with a jump and a twirl, the hare chases the tortoise. The other hares follow behind, shouting, "Run, run, run." The other animals continue shouting, "Go, tortoise, go."

The hare almost catches up, but the tortoise crosses the finish line to the delight of the cats and mice and goats, who all rush up, shouting, "You did it. You beat that hare. You won the race."

The hares slink up, and the other animals point an accusing finger at them and sing:

You Aren't the Best

(to the tune of "Three Blind Mice")

You aren't the best.
You aren't the best.
See how he (or she) won.
See how he (or she) won.
He (or She) moved better than any of you.
He's (or She's) better looking and smarter, too.
We wouldn't want to be any of you.
'Cuz you aren't the best. ❧

Setting the Stage

The stage area is set with bushes as props. Some are used as background for the start and finish line, which is in the middle of the stage. Other bushes are used midway for the spot where the hares nap.

Arrange the stage and audience space so the race can be run around or through the audience, whether you are putting on the play in a confined area such as a classroom or in a gymnasium or cafeteria. The race course is circular, allowing the spectators at the beginning to also be at the finish line.

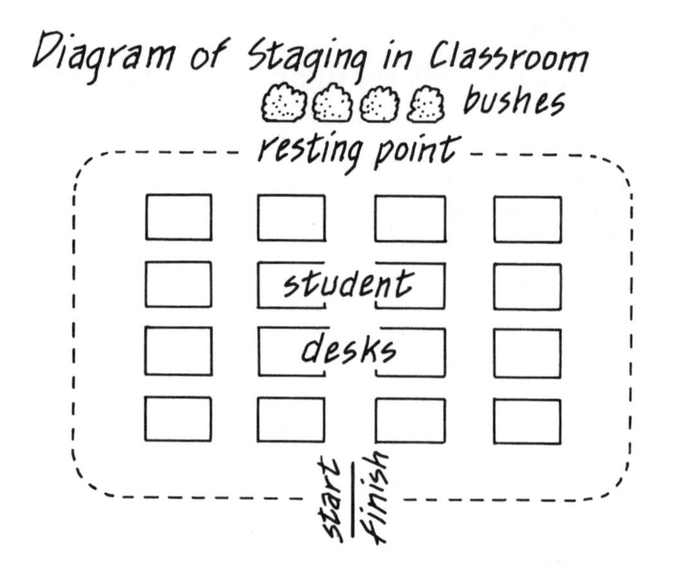

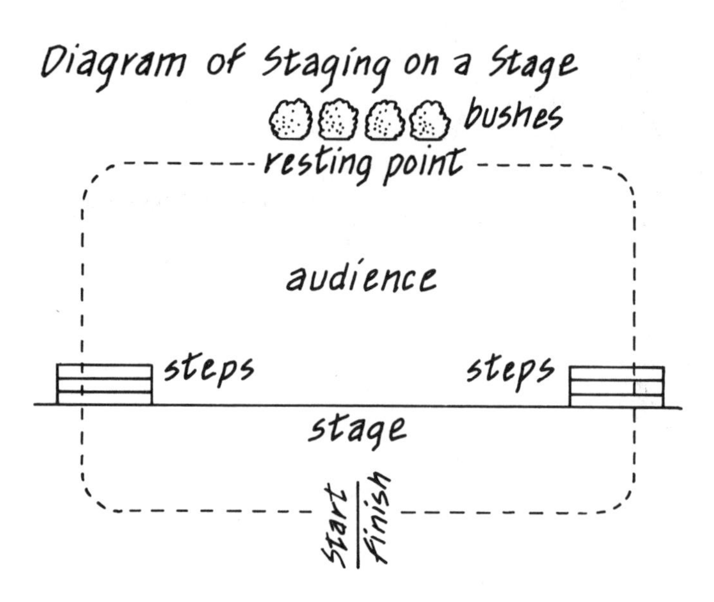

Movement Exercises

HARES

The most important element of the hares' movement is that it appear quick, almost nervous. To achieve this, the hares should bob up and down with their knees, appearing ready to hop off at any moment. When speaking, one hand should make a gesture, followed by the other hand doing the same thing.

To practice this, turn your students into hares and have them bob up and down, bending at the knees. Practicing the phrase "Yes, yes, we're the best," let them gesture, using alternate hands during the "yes, yes." The best effect will come from the knee-bending, and it may take some time for them to remember to do this continually. The hares bending at different times will give the look of activity to the entire group, so their knees need not wear out.

Reminding them to bob up and down and suggesting that some jump occasionally, feed them the lines of the lead hare, letting them respond with, "Yes, yes, we're the best."

"We hares are the best. We are the best animals."
"Yes, yes, we're the best."
"We are the smartest."
"Yes, yes, we're the best."
"We are the handsomest."
"Yes, yes, we're the best."
"We are the fastest."
"Yes, yes, we're the best."
While your students are hares, have them practice their running. The hares run a few steps, jump, and then run some more. Sometimes they will run, jump, and then twirl. Have them practice this the length of the practice area. Remind them that the point is not to reach the other end, but to do as many different variations as possible while getting there.

TORTOISES

Next, turn your actors into slowly plodding tortoises. The tortoise will be bent over, suggesting slowness. Each step will be an effort, and the foot comes down heavily, and the entire body leans into the step. Practice saying slowly and deliberately, "I . . . will . . . race . . . you." Then have your students walk the length of the practice area as the slow but steady tortoise.

WINNING AND LOSING

The only movements left to practice are the emotions of winning and losing. Let one student be the tortoise walking up to the finish line, to be patted on the back by the jumping and shouting animals. Then, in contrast, have your students practice how the hares will cross the finish line, dejected, with heads down, ears hanging, and shoulders drooping.

Play Read-through

Now read through the entire play, having the students take on the parts of all the characters as they appear.

Costumes and Props

- ❑ Hare masks (see pp. 73, 87, 88)
- ❑ Tortoise masks (see pp. 78, 94)
- ❑ Mouse masks (see pp. 76, 92)
- ❑ Lion masks (see pp. 75, 90)
- ❑ Sheep masks (see pp. 77, 93)
- ❑ Wolf masks (see pp. 79, 95)
- ❑ Dog masks (see pp. 72, 84, 85)
- ❑ Goat masks (see pp. 72, 86)
- ❑ Cat masks (see pp. 71, 83)
- ❑ Hen masks (see pp. 74, 89)
- ❑ Bushes (see p. 64)

The cast of supporters for the tortoise can be any combination of animals used in other plays, or simply other tortoises.

COSTUMES & PROPS

Bell
Bush
Fish
Fishing Pole
Flower
Net
River
Signs
Wheat
Cap
Cat Mask
Dog Mask
Goat Mask
Hare Mask
Little Red Hen Mask
Lion Mask
Monkey Mask
Mouse Mask
Sheep Mask
Tortoise Mask
Wolf Mask

BELL

Materials

Bell pattern

Shiny paper or paper painted gold or silver

Yarn or string

Directions

1. Trace and cut out the pattern on this page.
2. Put the yarn or string through the hole.

BELL PATTERN

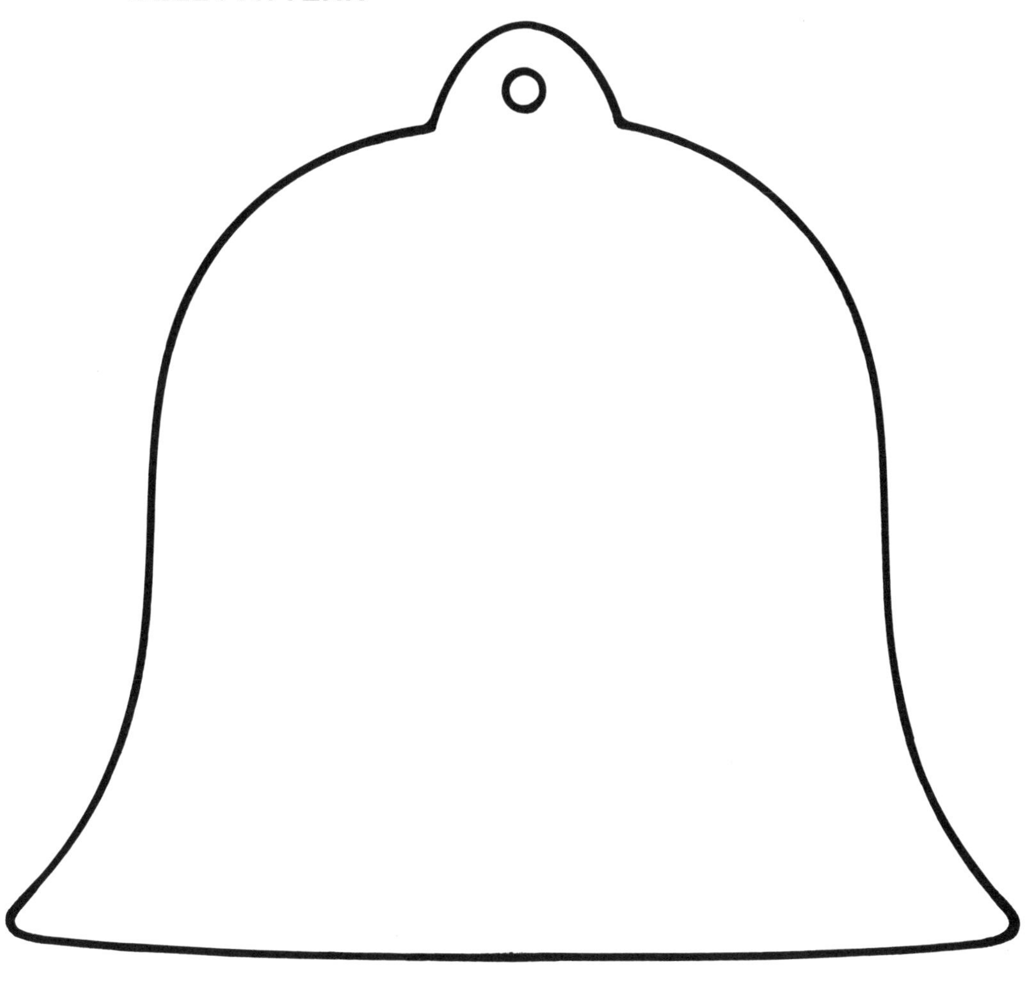

If you have a small bell you can hang on a string, you can use that instead.

BUSH

Materials

Sheet of green railroad board

Strip of tagboard, 3" x 24"

Student chair

Directions

1. Cut a bush shape out of railroad board, making bush as high and wide as sheet size will allow.
2. Staple tagboard strip horizontally, midway across the back of bush.
3. Slip tagboard strip attached to bush over back of chair.

Because bushes conceal actors, props, and even activity in most of the stories in this book, you'll want to make at least eight of them and store them in a place you won't forget, so they can be used again and again.

FISH

Materials

Fish pattern

Crayons, felt-tip pens, or paints

Directions

1. Duplicate the fish pattern (p. 82), making enough fish so each fisherman can catch at least two. (It would be sad to send the fishermen home with nothing.)
2. The fish can be decorated, back and front with crayons, felt-tip pens, or paints.

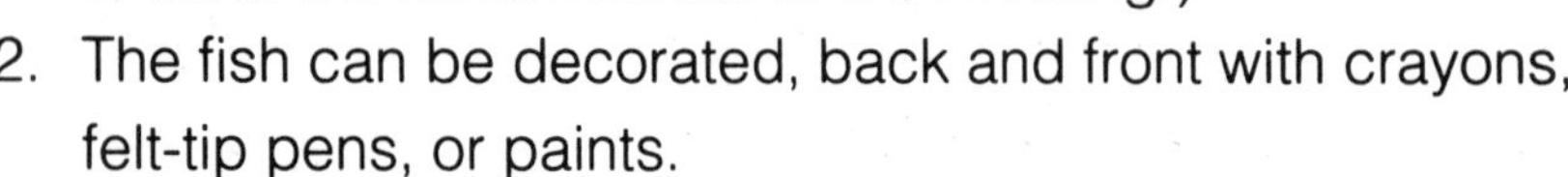

FISHING POLE

Materials

Yardsticks

Brown butcher paper

Rubber bands

String

Directions

1. For each pole, cut a length of brown butcher paper about 12" long.
2. Lay the yardstick on the long edge, and roll the butcher paper around the yardstick. See the diagram.
3. While holding the fishing pole, have a partner slip a rubber band around the end, middle, and tip.
4. Now, cut a piece of string the length of the pole and tie it on the end of the pole, or slip it under one of the rubber bands on the end to secure it.

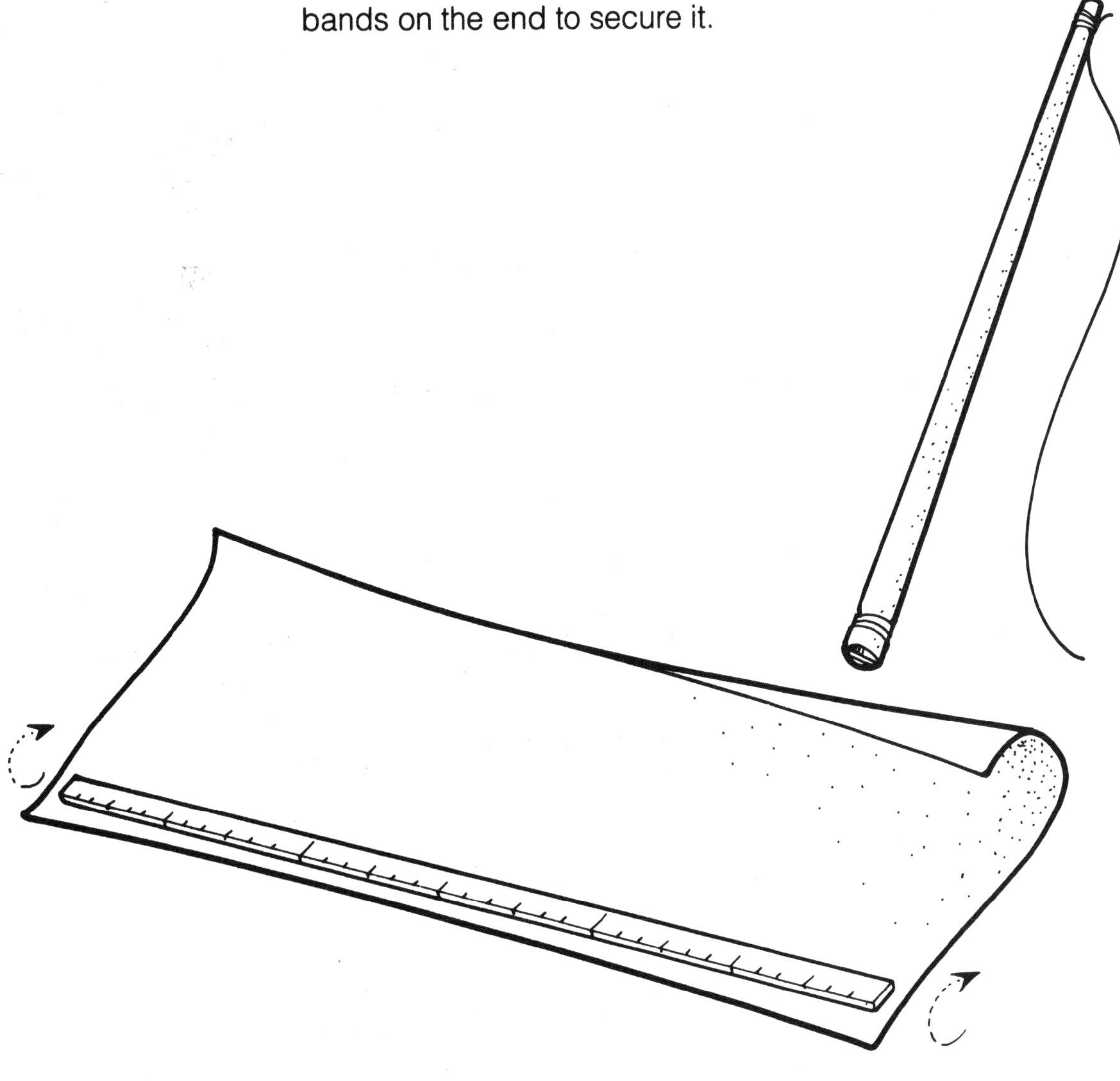

FLOWER

Materials

Flower pattern

Scrap paper in several colors

Directions

1. Trace and cut out the pattern on this page.
2. Pin or tape to city mice as corsages or boutonnieres.

FLOWER PATTERN

NET

Materials

White butcher paper, 36" x 36"

Directions

Remember paper snowflakes? This net uses the same principle.

1. Fold the paper in half and then in half again.
2. Then fold diagonally to form a triangle.
3. Cut alternately every inch from opposite ends of the fold. See illustration for proper angle. Don't cut strips all the way to one of the points; doing so will not make the "net" any bigger, only more unwieldy.
4. Unfold halfway until you are ready to use the net.
5. Because the net is ripped and bitten through by the mice and because it is very hard to fold back into carrying size, make an extra net to be used at the final rehearsal.

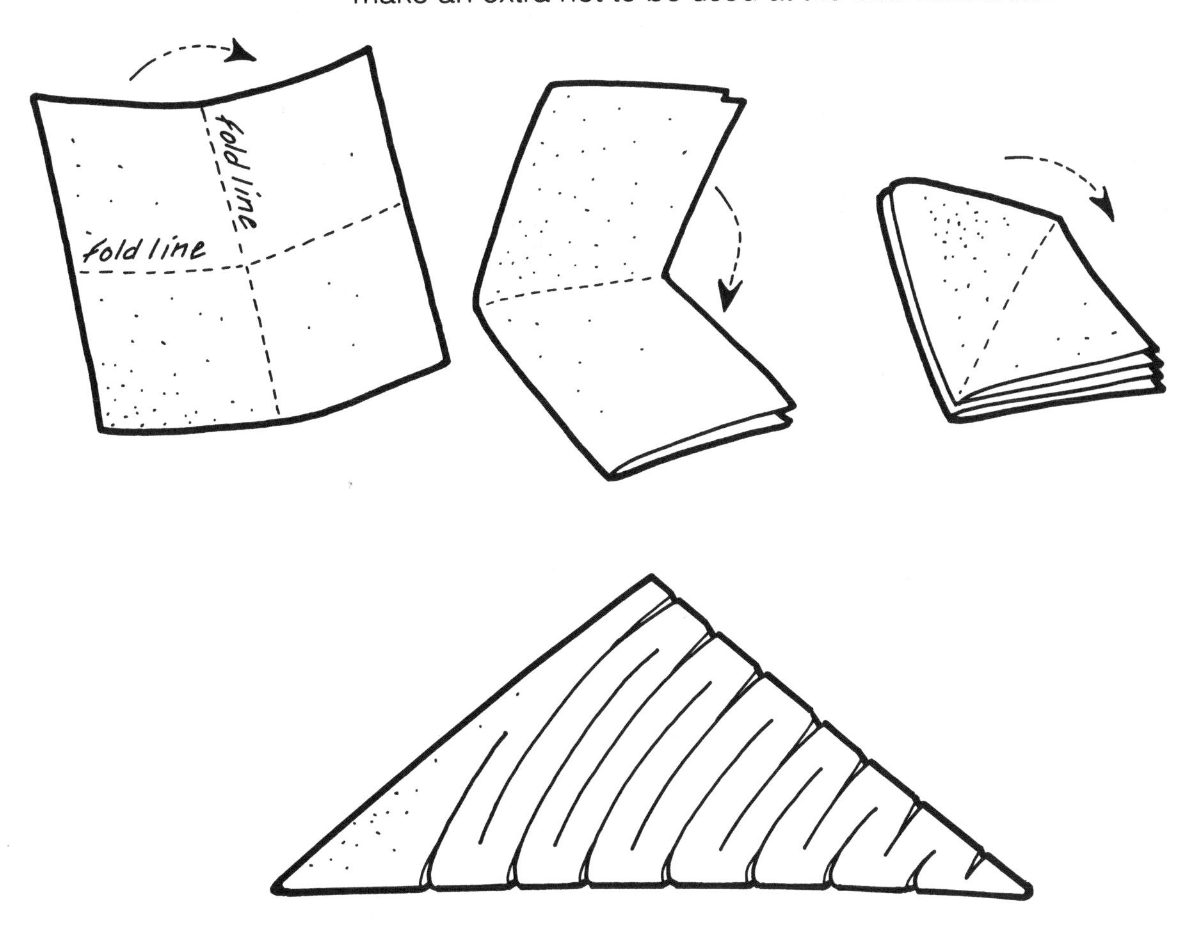

RIVER

Materials

Blue butcher paper

Directions

1. The river is one piece of butcher paper; cut as long as your stage area will permit.
2. The trick to this river is the slits. Make them about 12" long. Make as many as you have fishermen.
3. Hide the fish inside the slits with the heads barely sticking out so your fishermen can easily pull them out with their hands when they get a bite.
4. To be extra fancy, trim the sides of the river in a long wavy pattern to resemble the winding course a river might take.
5. You may find it helpful to tape this river to the floor so it does not pull when they are pulling fish from the river.

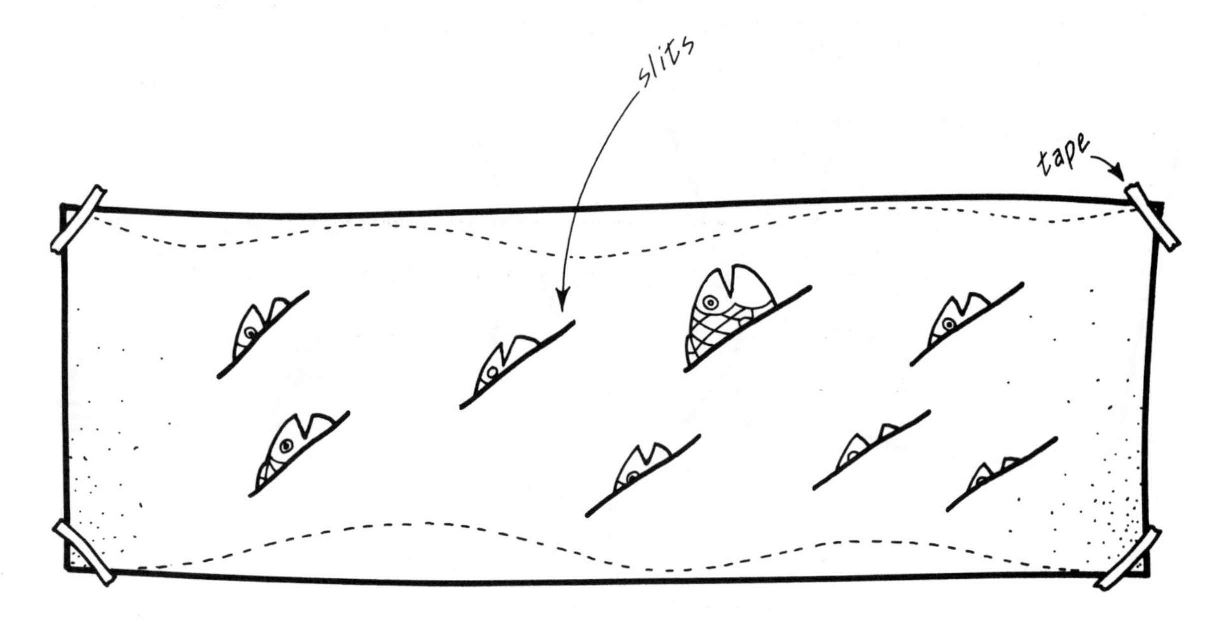

SIGNS

Materials

Tagboard or butcher paper
Wide felt-tip pens or paints
Stencil (optional)

Directions

1. Stencil the lesson of the story, or write it freehand on the paper. (It can also be printed out on a computer, if one is available.)
2. Roll up the sign in an inconspicuous place onstage (for example, in the mouse hole in "Belling the Cat"), ready to be unrolled at the conclusion of the play.

The lesson of the story for "The Shepherd Boy and the Wolf" is

"People Won't Believe Someone Who Always Tells Lies."

The lesson of the story for "Belling the Cat" is

"Some Things Are Easier Said Than Done."

WHEAT

Materials

Wheat pattern

Yellow construction paper

Yellow tagboard or railroad board sheets

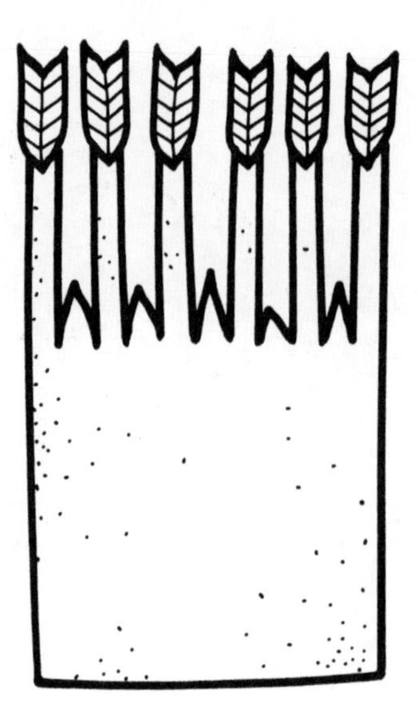

Directions

1. Duplicate the wheat pattern on this page on yellow construction paper and cut out.
2. Cut strips in the top third of a sheet of railroad board to form the stalks of wheat (see diagram). The remaining two-thirds will be used to lift the wheat field above the bushes.
3. Glue the wheat onto the stalks.

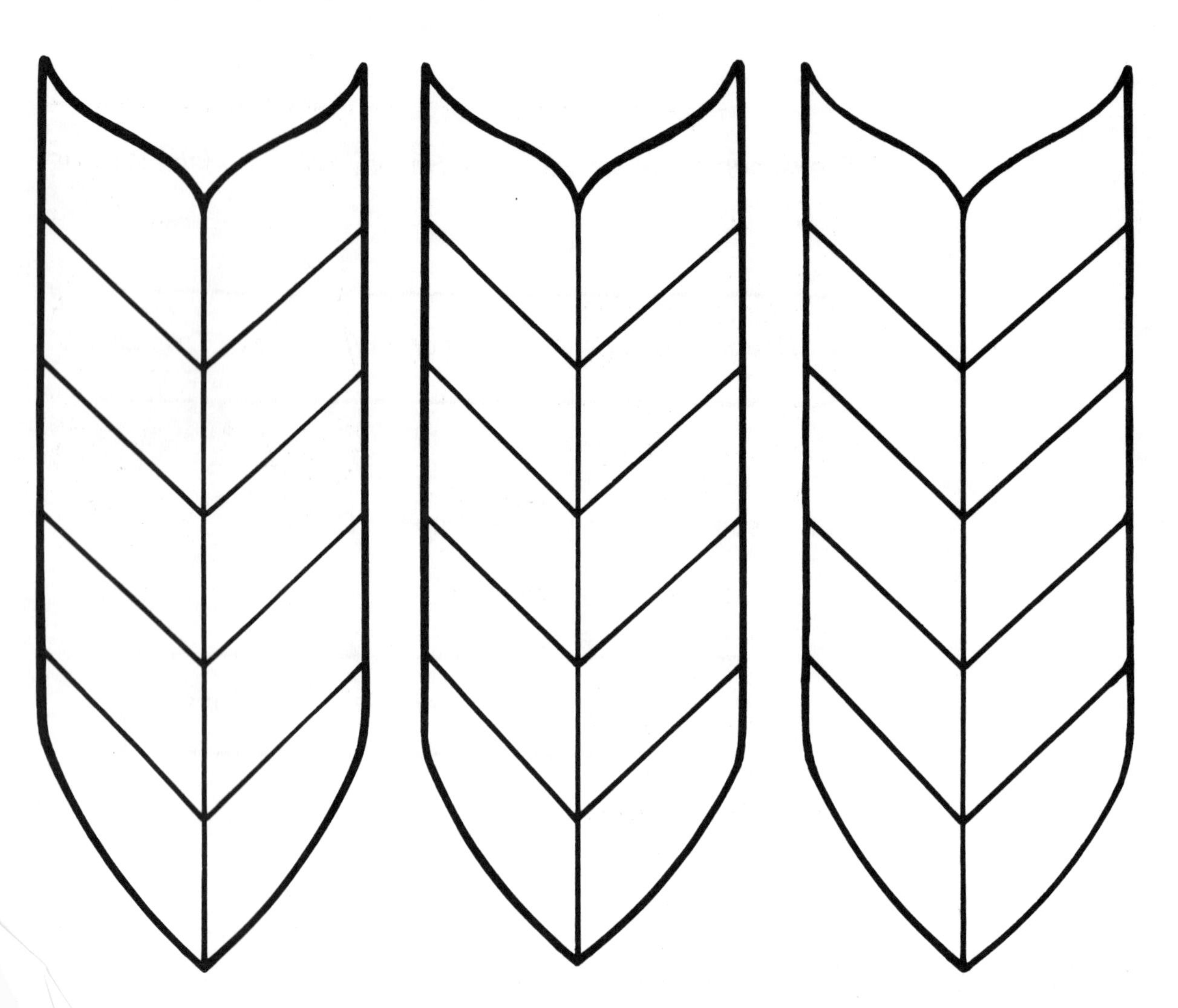

CAP

Materials

Cap pattern
Tagboard
Construction paper, 12" x 18", several colors

Directions

1. Trace cap pattern (p. 81) on tagboard, extending the two ends by 4" each. This will make a cap that can adjust to fit any size of head.
2. Trace around tagboard cap outline onto construction paper.
3. Cut out cap.
4. Fit a cap snugly around each child's head, and staple the ends together.

CAT

Materials

Cat mask pattern
Construction paper
Black paper scraps for whiskers
Crayons, felt-tip pens, or paints
Tagboard strips, 1-1/2" x 24"
Butcher paper for tail (optional)

Directions

1. Duplicate mask pattern (p. 83) on construction paper, or use pattern as a tracing or cutting guide.
2. Decorate mask with crayons, felt-tip pens, or paints.
3. Cut out mask.
4. Cut out eyeholes.
5. Cut out whiskers, and glue them onto mask.
6. Fit a tagboard strip around each child's head and staple ends of strip together.
7. Staple mask to tagboard headband.
8. If desired, cut a long strip of butcher paper for a tail, and tape or tuck inside back of belt.

DOG

Materials

Dog mask pattern (face and ears)
Brown construction paper
Black scrap paper for whiskers
Felt-tip pen or crayon
Tagboard strips, 1-1/2" x 24"

Directions

1. Duplicate face and ear patterns (pp. 84 and 85) on brown construction paper.
2. Cut out face and ears.
3. Cut out eyeholes.
4. Color the nose.
5. Color spots on muzzle for whiskers.
6. Glue ears onto mask. They are meant to flop, creating more motion as the dogs come bounding in and making them appear larger.
7. Fit a tagboard strip around each child's head, and staple ends of strip together.
8. Staple mask to tagboard headband.

GOAT

Materials

Goat mask pattern (face and ears)
Gray construction paper
White construction paper scraps for horns
Felt-tip pen or crayon
Tagboard strips, 1-1/2" x 24"

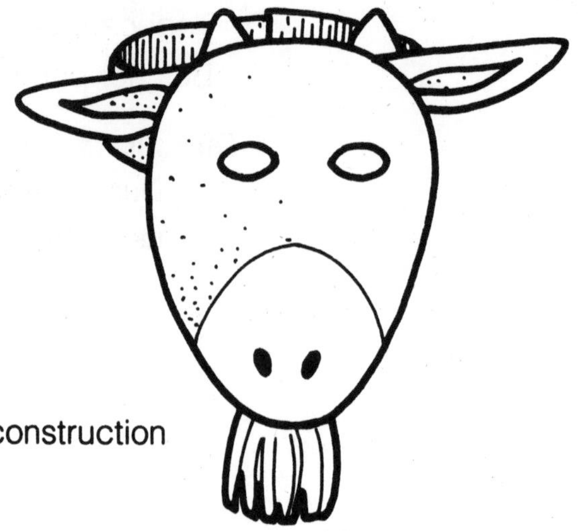

Directions

1. Duplicate mask pattern (p. 86) on gray construction paper.
2. Cut out face and ears.
3. Cut the fringe at bottom of face, which is the beard.
4. Cut out eyeholes.
5. Color the nose.

(continued on next page)

6. Color insides of ears, and glue ears onto mask so they stick out at the sides.
7. Cut triangles from white construction paper for horns, and glue them on back of mask.
8. Fit a tagboard strip around each child's head, and staple ends of strip together.
9. Staple mask to tagboard headband.

HARE

Materials

Hare mask pattern (face and ears)
Gray and pink construction paper
Black and white paper scraps
Felt-tip pen or crayon
Tagboard strips, 1-1/2" x 24"

Directions

1. Duplicate face and ears patterns (pp. 87 and 88) on gray construction paper.
2. Cut out face and ears.
3. Cut pink inserts for ears, and glue them in place.
4. Cut a pink circle for nose.
5. Draw line for hare's smile.
6. Cut long whiskers from black paper.
7. Cut out two white teeth to fit under hare's smile.
8. Glue pieces onto mask.
9. Fit a tagboard strip around child's head, and staple ends of strip together.
10. Staple mask to tagboard headband.

LITTLE RED HEN

Materials

Little Red Hen mask pattern

Red, orange, and yellow construction paper

Tagboard strips, 1-1/2" x 24"

Directions

1. Duplicate mask pattern (p. 89).
2. Staple pattern pieces to corresponding colors of construction paper.
3. Cut out pattern pieces, and unstaple them from construction paper.
4. Cut a yellow 2" x 2" square for beak. Fold square diagonally, and draw two holes on top flap.
5. Cut out eyeholes.
6. Glue pieces onto mask according to diagram. To attach beak, glue bottom triangle to mask.
7. Fit a tagboard strip around each child's head, and staple ends of strip together.
8. Staple mask to tagboard headband.

LION

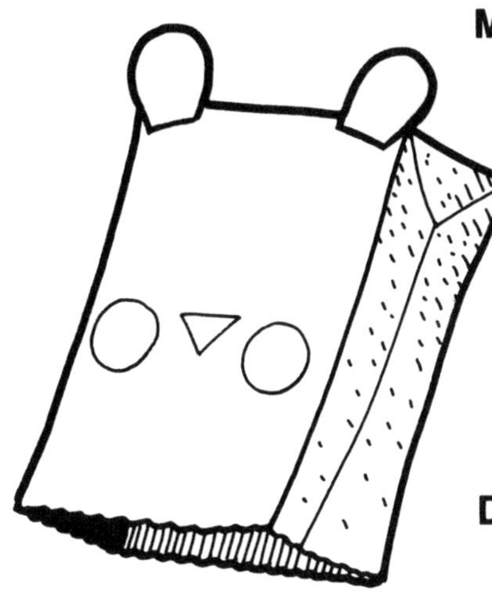

Materials

Lion features pattern
Large grocery sack
Orange, yellow, and black construction paper
Strips of yellow and orange construction paper for mane, 1-1/2" x 6"
Wide felt-tip pen
Butcher paper for tail (optional)

Directions

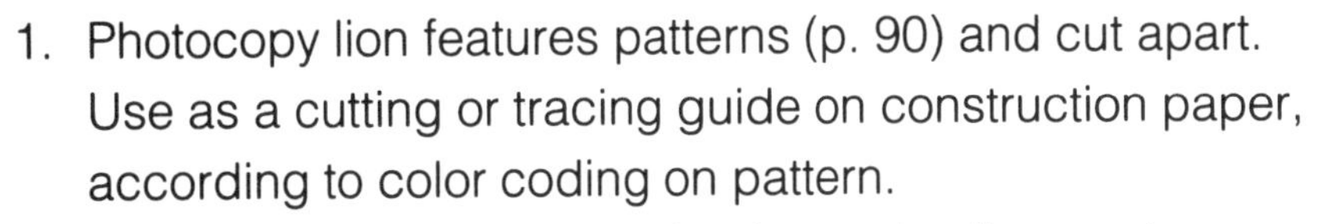

1. Photocopy lion features patterns (p. 90) and cut apart. Use as a cutting or tracing guide on construction paper, according to color coding on pattern.
2. Glue yellow ears, orange cheeks, and yellow and orange nose parts to front of paper-sack mask. (The mask is made on the entire sack, making the lion look extra big.)
3. Using a wide felt-tip pen, draw eyes and mouth according to diagram.
4. Cut out eyeholes, leaving a rim of ink to emphasize eyes.
5. Cut whiskers from black construction paper, and glue them on top of orange cheek circles.
6. For mane, glue yellow and orange strips around face as shown in illustration.
7. Cut an armhole on each side of sack, and tape each one around inside edge to prevent ripping.
8. If desired, cut a long strip of butcher paper for a tail, and attach it to the back of sack.

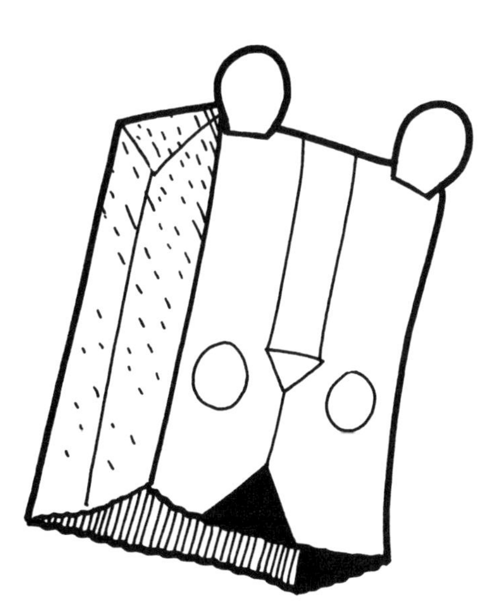

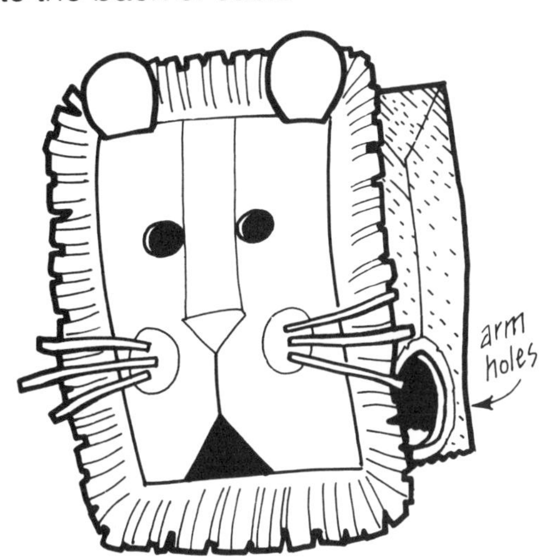

MONKEY

Materials

Monkey mask pattern
Brown construction paper
Felt-tip pen or crayon
Tagboard strips, 1-1/2" x 24"

Directions

1. Duplicate monkey mask (p. 91) on brown paper.
2. Cut out mask.
3. Cut out eyeholes.
4. Draw in lines on face.
5. Fit a tagboard strip around each child's head, and staple ends of strip together.
6. Staple mask to tagboard headband.

MOUSE

Materials

Mouse mask pattern (face and ears)
Gray or white construction paper
Tagboard strips, 1-1/2" x 24"
Black paper scraps for whiskers
Crayons, felt-tip pens, or paints (optional)
Black butcher paper for tail (optional)

Directions

1. Duplicate mask (p. 92) on gray construction paper (to eliminate need to color) or on white construction paper (if you want children to decorate masks). Or use pattern for a tracing or cutting guide.
2. Cut out and glue ears onto mask.
3. Cut out eyeholes.
4. Cut out and glue whiskers onto mask.
5. Fit a tagboard strip around each child's head, and staple ends of strip together.
6. Attach mouse mask to tagboard strip.
7. If desired, cut a long strip from butcher paper for a tail, and tape or tuck it inside back of belt.

SHEEP

Materials

Sheep mask pattern (face and ears)

Black and pink construction paper

Cotton balls

Tagboard strips, 1-1/2" x 24"

Directions

1. Photocopy mask (p. 93) and staple it to black construction paper. (Cotton "wool" shows up best in contrast with black mask.)
2. Cut out face and ears.
3. Cut out eyeholes before unstapling pattern from construction paper.
4. Glue ears onto mask.
5. Cut out two small pink circles (a paper punch will do) for the nose.
6. Stretch and glue some cotton balls on top edge of the mask for the wool.
7. Fit a tagboard strip around each child's head, and staple ends of strip together.
8. Staple mask to tagboard headband.

TORTOISE

Materials

Tortoise mask pattern
Green construction paper
White paper scraps
Green butcher paper
Black or brown paint or felt-tip pens
Tagboard strips, 1-1/2" x 24"

Directions

1. Duplicate mask (p. 94) on green construction paper.
2. Cut out mask.
3. Outline mouth and wrinkles with paint or pen.
4. Cut out eyeholes.
5. Rim eyeholes with white circles for emphasis. To ensure symmetry, put two pieces of white scrap paper together and cut circle larger than eyeholes. Put the two circles under eyeholes and trace. Cut eyeholes in circles. Glue circles around eyeholes.
6. For shell, cut a large circle (about 24" diameter) from green butcher paper. Using black or brown paint or felt-tip pens, make concentric circles with connecting lines to form shell pattern.
7. Fit a tagboard strip around each child's head, and staple ends of strip together.
8. Attach mask on one side of tagboard headband and shell on the other side to cover child's back. If desired, fit another tagboard strip around waist and attach strip to inside of shell.

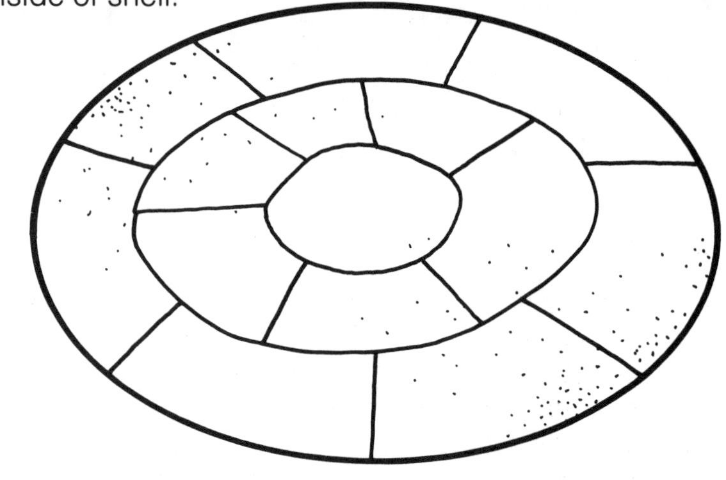

WOLF

Materials

Wolf mask pattern

Brown or gray construction paper

Felt-tip pen or crayon

Tagboard strips, 1-1/2" x 24"

Directions

1. Duplicate mask pattern (p. 95) on brown or gray construction paper.
2. Cut out face and ears.
3. Trace lines on face and around eyes to emphasize, and color in nose.
4. Cut out eyeholes.
5. Cut whiskers and glue to mask.
6. Cut ears and glue to mask.
7. Fit a tagboard strip around each child's head, and staple ends of strip together.
8. Staple mask to tagboard headband.

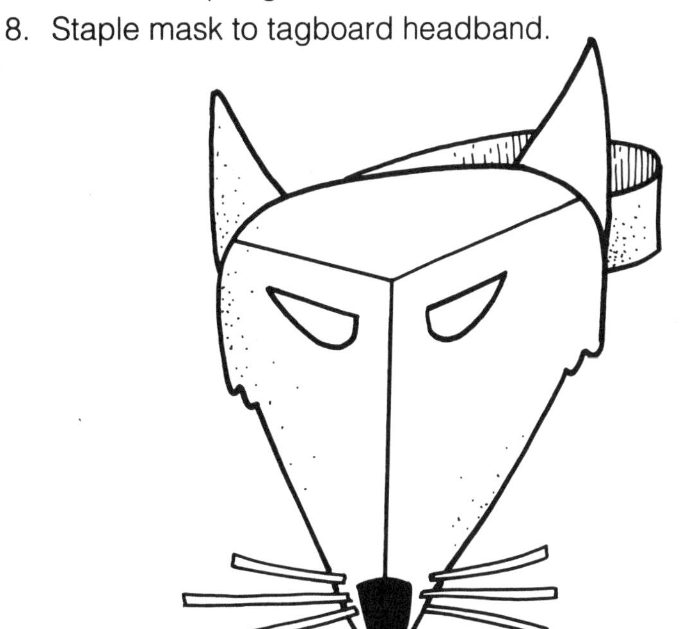

Wolf's Disguise ("The Wolf and the Little Kids")

When the wolf returns the third time, his paws must be whitened to fool the wary goats. To do this, the wolf can dip his feet and hands in a container of flour as the story suggests, or he can put oversized white socks over the front part of his shoes and white gloves over his hands.

PATTERNS

Cap Pattern
Fish Pattern
Cat Mask
Dog Mask
Goat Mask
Hare Mask
Little Red Hen Mask
Lion Features
Monkey Mask
Mouse Mask
Sheep Mask
Tortoise Mask
Wolf Mask

Cap Pattern

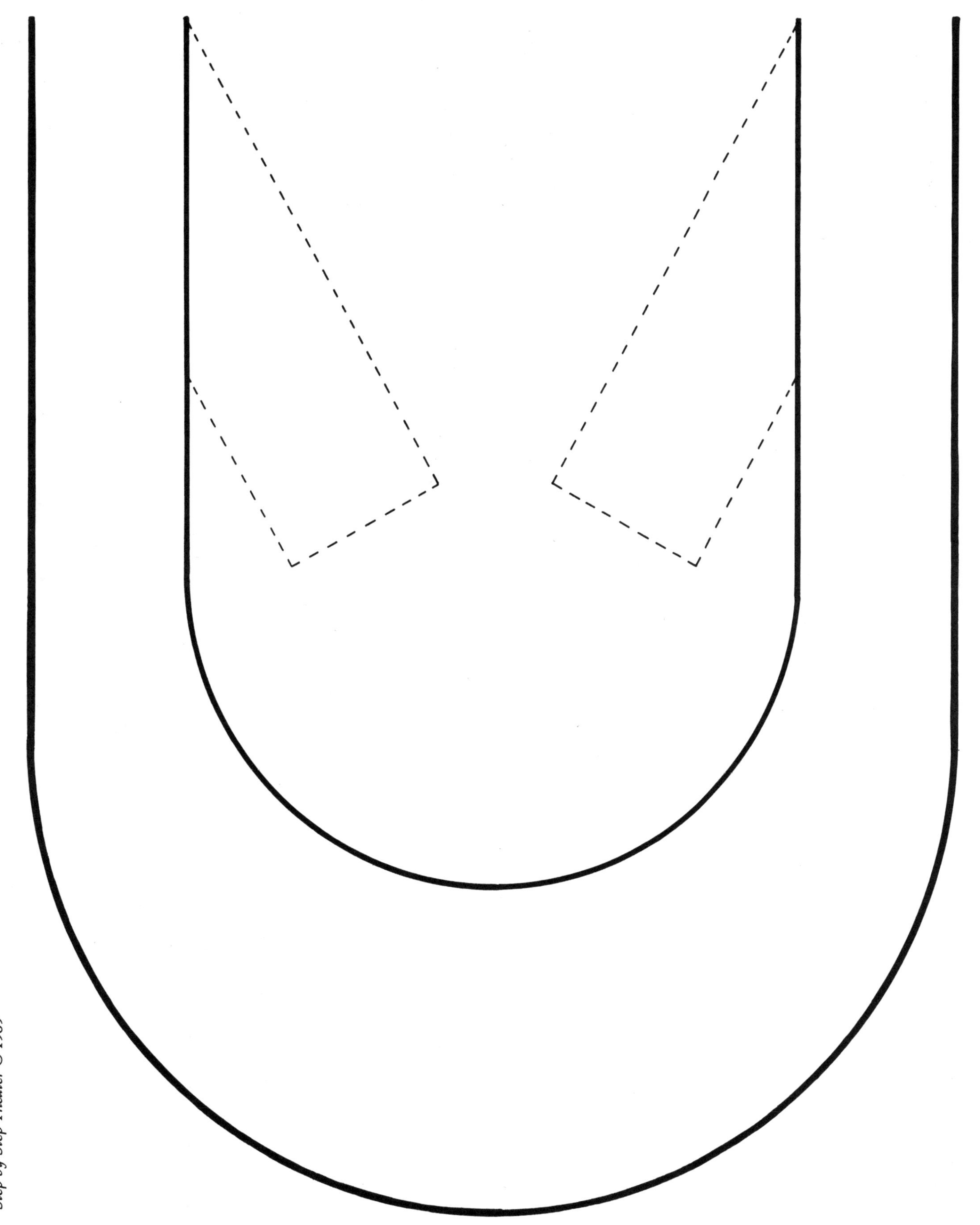

Fish Pattern

Cat Mask

Dog Mask: Face

Dog Mask: Ears

Goat Mask

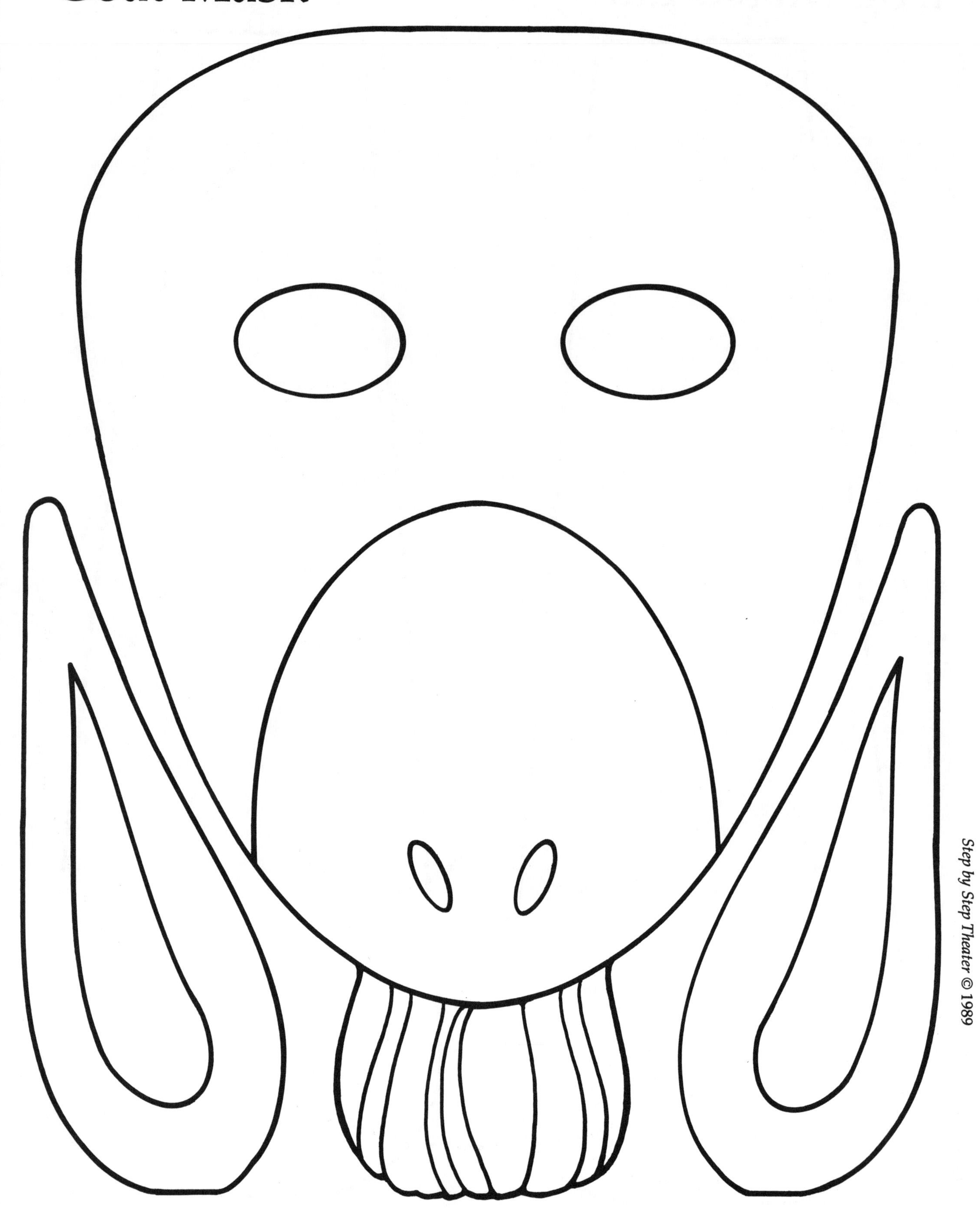

Hare Mask: Face

Hare Mask: Ears

Little Red Hen Mask

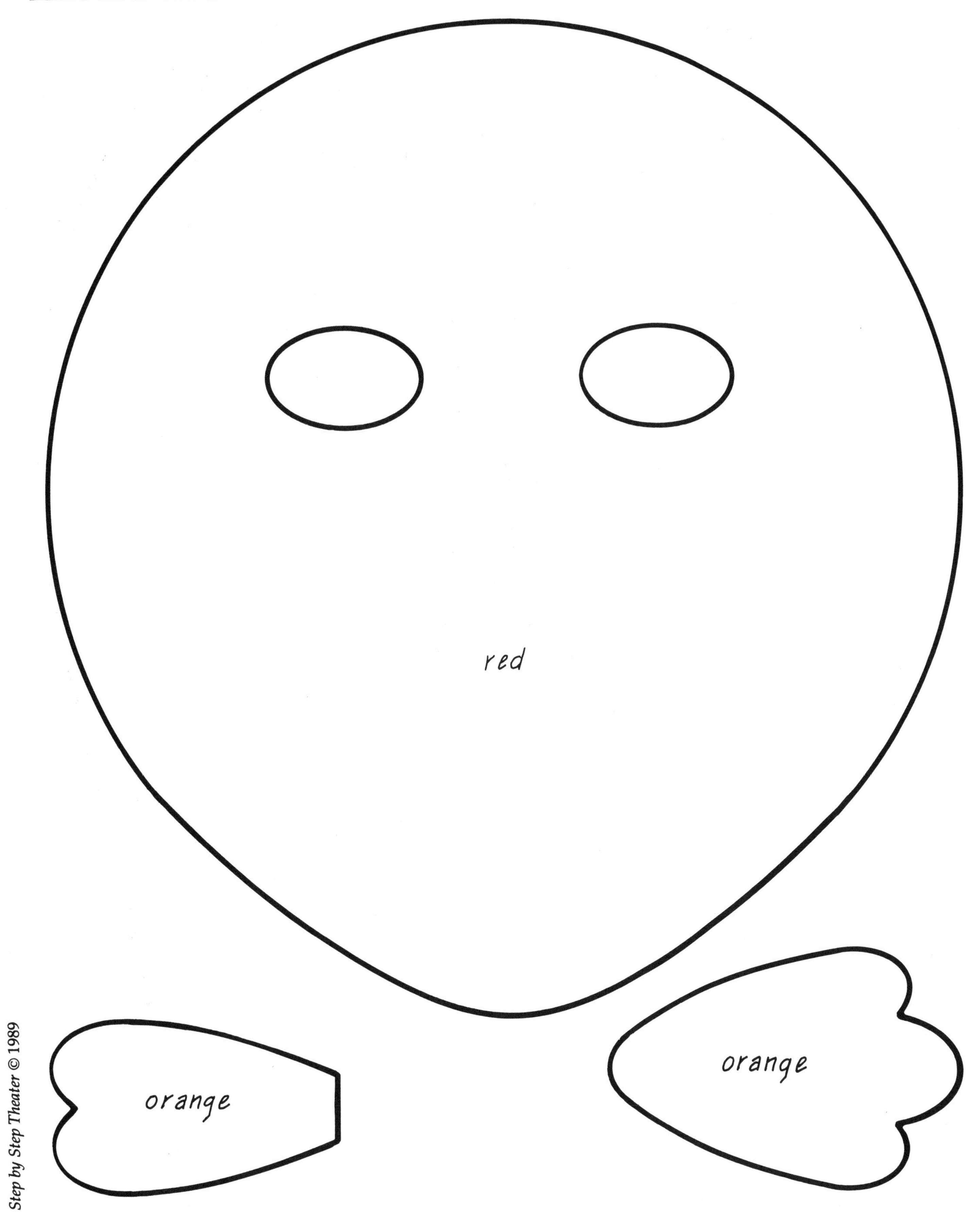

Lion Features

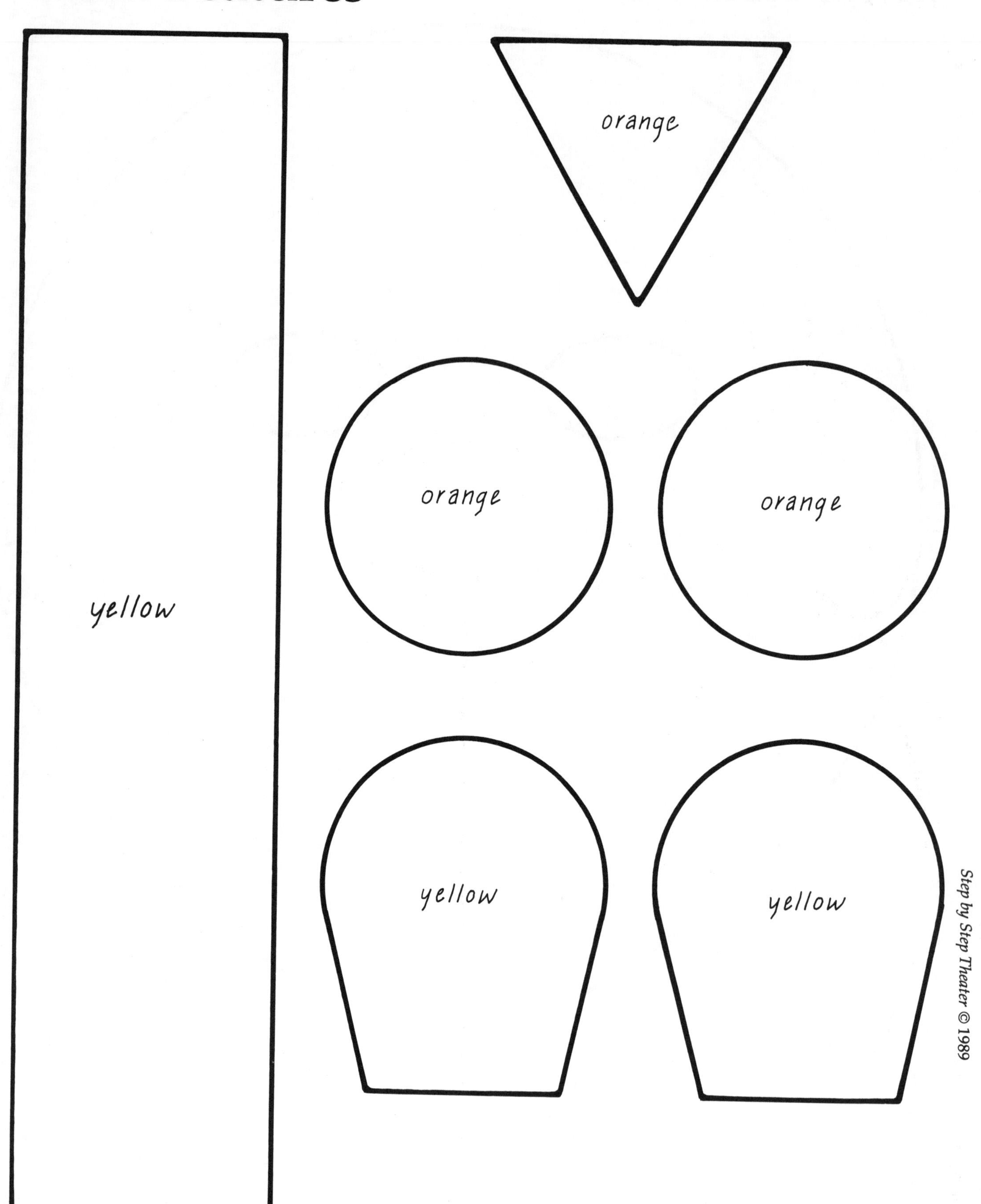

Monkey Mask

Mouse Mask

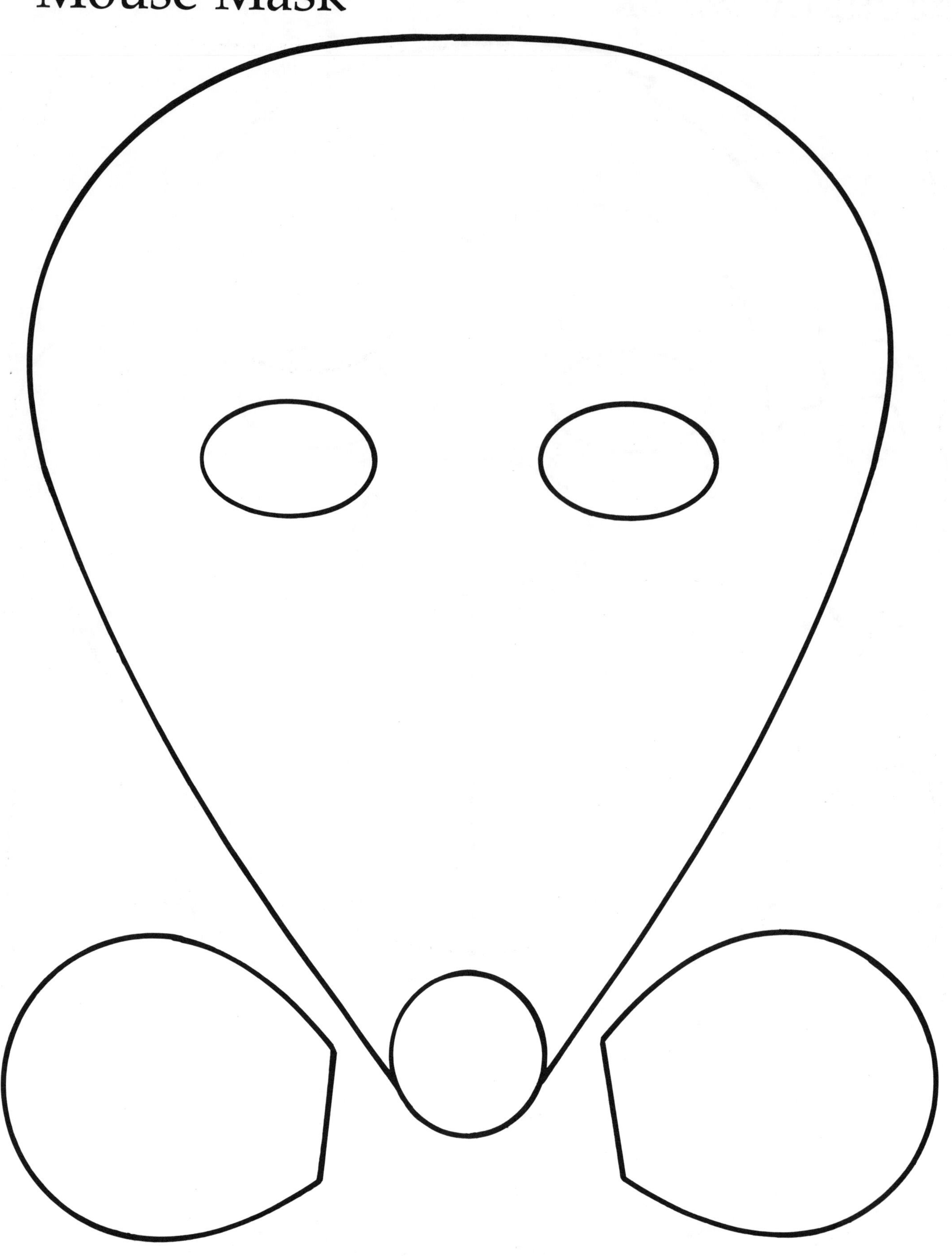

Sheep Mask

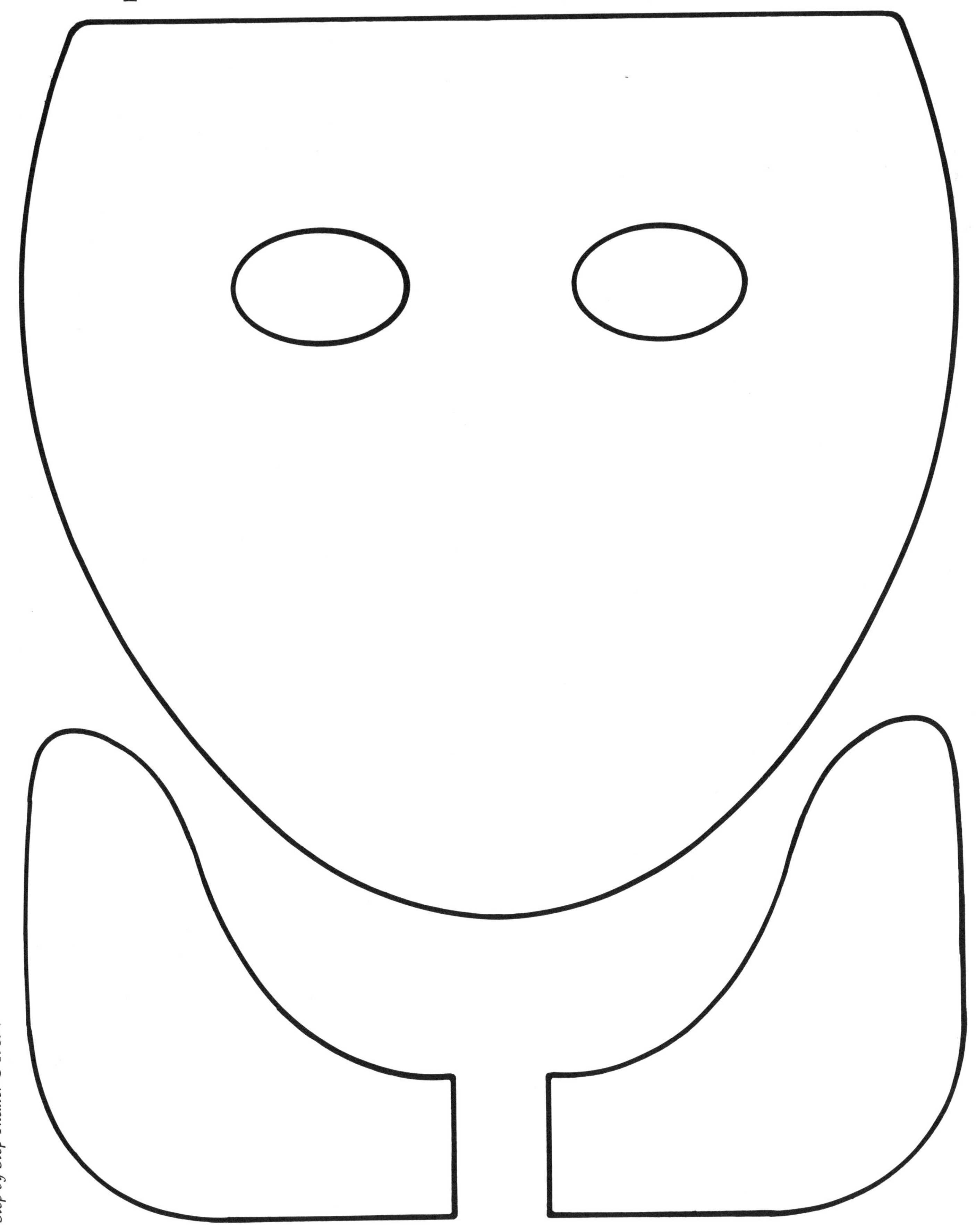

Tortoise Mask

Wolf Mask

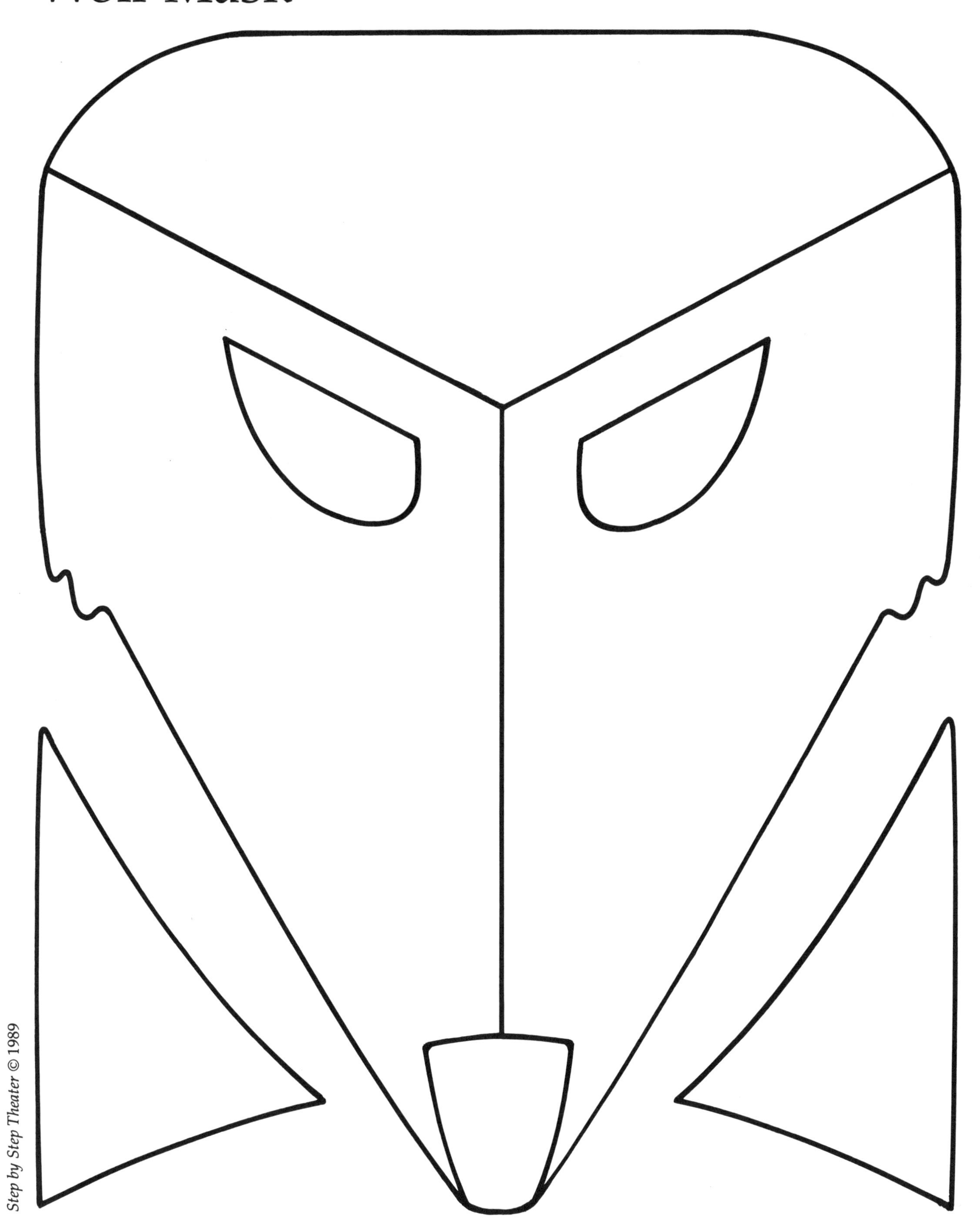

The End